I Am

NICK JONES

YOUCAXTON PUBLICATIONS

OXFORD & SHREWSBURY

ISBN 978-1-912419-80-7
Printed and bound in Great Britain.
Published by YouCaxton Publications 2019
YCBN: 01

YouCaxton Publications

enquiries@youcaxton.co.uk

Contents

Acknowledgements

I AM INDEBTED TO: Anthony Keith Uniforms; Bedfordshire Police Historical & Museum Society; Bristol Tourist Information Centre; British Transport Police; The College of Policing; Lorna Fergusson; The Franciscan Sisters of Christian Charity; Great Western Railways; Guildhall School of Music; the International Consortium of Investigative Journalists; Invacare UK; Ali Luke; Luton Airport London; Network Rail; the Royal Engineers Association; Stanbrook Abbey; the Swiss Government's Tourism Office; Sue Thorogood; and Visionmetric. Also to Tee Blake (graphic design), Sarah Classick (fashion advice); Sasha Lubetkin (copy editing, proof reading and invaluable suggestions and encouragement); Ted Stevens (reader); and David Williams (police procedural advice and information).

To keep up to date with Nick Jones' novels visit:
www.ampersandworld.co.uk

PROLOGUE

Barbican, City of London

'YOU TELL 'EM, Nige!' yelled the taxi driver.

The distinctive *basso profundo* voice of Nigel Farage boomed inside the interior of the taxi, as the black London cab pulled to a halt in front of one of the tall Barbican towers. "Immigration control MUST be the country's number one priority!"

It was just after 6 o'clock on a bleak spring evening. Light rain was falling.

The shaven-headed driver half-turned to address his passenger in the back. ''Ere we are lady. Churchill Tower. Wasn't so bad was it, considering the traffic? That Euston Road underpass is always terrible this time of day.' He pushed his right arm out of the window to release the handle of the rear door, but made no attempt to help his passenger alight.

Dressed entirely in black, Marta Kashani remained motionless. Twisting in her seat, she gazed upwards through the rear window but couldn't even see the top of the tower. The driver gave the door handle a sharp jab and the door swung open. 'Card or cash?' he asked.

'Please?' She remained bolt upright on the edge of the seat, clutching her handbag in her lap.

'Wanna pay wiv plastic or cash?'

'Can I give you euros please?'

''fraid not lady. Pounds sterling only. We're just about to quit Europe. 'ain't you 'eard?'

'So how much please?'

'£84 on the meter.'

After some moments the woman managed to collect together four £20 notes and two £2 coins. She passed it to the driver through the slot in the dividing screen. Still he made no effort to help her to alight. The Farage barrage had been replaced with an ancient rock anthem by Queen, followed by an advertisement for car insurance for the over 60s. The lady cautiously eased herself out onto the wet cobbles, to find her overnight case lying on its side on the pavement.

'Now you 'ave yerself a lovely day and mind you don't go tripping over on that kerb!' The black cab executed a 180 degree turn and sped off down Spice Lane in a flurry of blue diesel fumes.

Churchill Tower loomed menacingly above, its exposed concrete walls glistening in the rain. Marta had never seen such a tall structure. Picking up her case, she approached the brightly-lit entrance foyer. The automatic doors slid back silently.

Inside, the main reception was generously large, with white-painted walls and long stacks of maple bookcases. The furniture was of Scandinavian style, set on a deep-pile carpet of papal purple. The newcomer could hardly fail to notice the cosmopolitan nature of the residents and visitors in the foyer of Churchill Tower. A large black lady, wearing a bright orange turban, was leading two youngsters towards the entrance door; while, seated on a long sofa, reading a copy of *The Times*, was a city businessman in a three-piece suit.

In front of a broad picture window which looked out onto a paved courtyard and an ornamental pool, was a curved reception desk presided over by a stocky black security guard. He eyed the visitor suspiciously from behind his sunglasses. A City of London identification badge, hanging on a striped lanyard, labelled him as Malcolm (though residents privately referred to him as "Malcolm X"). Looking down onto his reception desk, from matching alcoves, were portrait photos of Britain's wartime Prime Minister and a bearskin-wearing Queen Elizabeth, seated side-saddle on a horse.

With his stout muscular arms spread across the desk, Malcolm peered quizzically over the rims of his aviator glasses. What he saw was a dark-skinned middle-aged woman, wearing a layered black skirt reaching to the floor, with black net half-gloves and a tiny black pillbox hat with a short black mesh veil. 'Please, I have come to visit Mr Kashani,' she whispered.

The guard casually reached for his tabulated clipboard. 'Is he expecting you?'

'Yes he is.'

Malcolm entered the date and time of the woman's arrival, alongside 'Apt 37B.' He held out a ballpoint pen. 'Sign here please.'

In the column marked 'Visitor's signature' Marta simply wrote 'K', though it might just as easily have been an 'X'.

The guard retrieved his clipboard. 'I'll take you through to the lift lobby. Follow me.' Courtesy wasn't Malcolm's strong suit. He led the way across the purple carpet, making no attempt to help the woman with her luggage.

They entered a dimly-lit triangular vestibule. The floor covering had now becomes a bilious orange and the subdued lighting was from stainless steel up-lighters. Pairs of windowless steel doors were set in the centre of each of the three cream-coloured walls. In the middle of the carpeted triangle was a squat, free-standing green cylinder, surmounted by a stainless steel cone. Marta assumed if it was a drinking fountain.

The hulk approached the strange metal object and pushed a button in the rim of the cone. After a short pause there was an electronic 'ping' and one of the pairs of lift doors slid open. Malcolm nodded to the woman to enter. The lift car was extremely small, with barely space for six standing figures. Unaided, she dragged her valise in behind her. Pointing to a long list of numbered buttons running from 1 to 43 the guard mumbled: 'When the doors close, press 37.

Mr Kashani will be waiting for you on the landing'. The doors slid shut and the lift car started its noiseless ascent.

Inside, the lift car was a claustrophobic windowless space. Marta – who rarely rode in elevators - was relieved that no-one else got in as it climbed uninterrupted to the 37th floor. It slowed then juddered to a halt. The doors opened to reveal an identical lift lobby to the one she had just left, complete with the same orange carpet and another circular 'drinking fountain'.

In the cleft of one of the lobby's angles was an opened front door, spilling light outwards. Framed by the doorway was a portly figure dressed in a black jacket and neatly-pressed pin-striped trousers over polished black brogue shoes. Over his crisp white shirt the man sported a silk tie with red zig-zags over a blue ground. This, Marta Kashani recalled, was her estranged husband's 'signature neckwear'.

The bald-headed man facing her was clean-shaven and wore gold-framed glasses, which slightly emphasised the sinister appearance of his hooded eyes. Marta was aware that he wore a corset, though whether for reasons of vanity or sexual perversion she had never been able to discern. After an absence of three years he still looked vain.

Aamir Kashani gave the woman a benign smile of welcome and stepped forward, taking both her hands in his. 'Marta, my dear. How good to see you.' He lifted her case and led the way into the apartment. 'Do come in.'

They stepped into the small entrance lobby of the apartment, off which was a narrow galley-type kitchen area. He pushed the front door shut and set her bag down. 'How was your flight?'

'Crowded and noisy. And the food was terrible.'

'Oh dear, how unfortunate. I am sorry I couldn't get my driver to come out to collect you, but he was returning from a military reunion in the Midlands. Can I make you some tea? Or perhaps you would prefer coffee?'

'Coffee would be nice, Aamir. May I just freshen up in your bathroom?'

'But of course. Along the passageway – the last door on the right. I'll have your coffee waiting for you in the salon.'

Several minutes later the woman shuffled nervously into Aamir Kashani's well-furnished sitting room. Antique rugs were scattered around the mahogany furniture. Across one whole side of the long room was a picture window looking out over the City of London. She had never seen such a dramatic panorama. Adopting the same pose as he had at the front door, the man stood with his back to the window. 'Perhaps you would like to step out onto the balcony to get a better view? You can see St Paul's Cathedral from up here. It is truly magnificent by night.'

'I'd prefer to see Etna.'

Despite Kashani's emollient manner, his wife remained taciturn in his domineering presence. Mixed feelings of grief and bewilderment were etched into her face. He gestured towards a brass tea trolley with a flourish worthy of the maitre d'hôtel at The Savoy. 'Do please help yourself to cream and sugar.'

She took a seat at the end of a long black leather sofa, bemused by the aerial view of night-time London. Centre stage – running across the room - was a magnificent early Caucasian Ushak, in rich ochres and ambers, all of six metres long. Its geometric precision perfectly matched the angularity of the apartment. She looked idly around, noting the pared-back modernity of the interior. A number of framed oil paintings hung along the back wall. Though her knowledge of the Impressionists was limited, she was pretty certain one of them was a Cezanne.

'Is this building very old?

'By City of London standards, no – only about 50 years. The whole Barbican Estate was built on war-damaged land in the 1960s. Its architectural style is known as 'brutalism".'

She sipped her coffee and sniffed. 'How appropriate.'

He remained standing at the window, like an un-wanted tourist guide. He gave a nervous cough. 'Right, I shall start at the beginning.

'Alice had been unwell for some days, complaining of headaches and eating very little. She was absent from school for a whole week. So I asked my private physician to call and give her a full examination. He took blood and saliva samples and said he would telephone me from the laboratory. Several hours later he called to say that the lab had made a positive diagnosis of chronic leukaemia and that our daughter needed to be admitted to a special clinic as soon as possible. Through contacts I have with certain Saudi business people, I was able to get her a private room in a clinic in St John's Wood. It's the best in London.'

Kashani moved away from the window to take a seat in an armchair opposite the sofa. He pulled a silk handkerchief from his breast pocket and dabbed his brow. 'Alice couldn't cope with the treatment the clinic was administering. Her body kept rejecting the tablets, poor thing. She was about to begin a course of chemotherapy, but then went into a rapid decline. They did everything possible to save her, but she died a fortnight later.' He carefully folded the handkerchief and replaced it in the top pocket of his jacket.

She was shocked by his description of the events: of the last days of their daughter. She carefully placed her coffee cup on the trolley. Pursing her lips she nodded sagely. 'I'm sure you did everything you could, Aamir.'

He sighed. 'It has been a terrible few weeks, I can tell you. The worst since your second miscarriage and our decision to separate. Only the week before she fell ill, Alice had heard that she had won a scholarship to the Guildhall School of Music, here in the Barbican.' He stood up and walked over to the window. 'The staff at the St John's Wood clinic were wonderful. They made all the arrangements for a small private ceremony in their chapel, which was followed by the cremation.'

'Were any of her friends from school at the ceremony?'

'None.' The reply was brusque, sounding as if he hadn't wanted to share his grief. 'I placed an announcement in *The Times* the following day. There's a garden of remembrance here in the Barbican,' he said, nodding to the landscaped piazza far below. 'I intend to have a simple plaque made and I shall place flowers on it each week. I will send you a photograph.'

After a long pause she asked: 'So now you are alone?'

He sighed and nodded. 'Yes. Fortunately, my work is keeping me very occupied at the moment.'

Kashani's wife looked around the room. It was lavishly furnished. The profusion of expensive rugs, the showy mahogany furniture and the collection of oil paintings indicated a comfortable lifestyle. Standing in a line along the long window shelf were three small bronze figures, each set on marble stands. The most distinctive was a warrior pulling back the copper string of a huge bow loaded with a bronze arrow. His back and chest were protected by an intricate armoured jacket, formed of small inter-laced copper panels, which overlapped like fish scales.

'And are you still dealing in oriental carpets and rugs?'

He shrugged. 'For the moment. But I don't know for how much longer.'

'Why so, Aamir?'

He got up and poured himself a half-cup of coffee. She declined a refill. 'My main trade has always been in tribal pieces from Afghanistan, which we import via Pakistan. My father taught me everything I know about carpets and rugs. But lately the Taliban has been regrouping and exerting much more power again, especially behind the scenes in the government. Now it's far too risky for me to go out there, even with a local bodyguard. So I've started to diversify.' He went to the window ledge and gently lifted the bowman. 'Into antiquities. Most are from the Mesopotamian period. I have a good contact in Baghdad.' He lovingly studied the bowman's figure. 'There's quite a market for special small pieces like this in London at the moment, with all the Iraqis and Saudis who have moved here.' He replaced the bowman on the shelf. 'Not to mention the Russians.'

'Now I'm sure you would like to take some of Alice's things back to Sicily as mementoes. Let me show you her bedroom and you can make your choice. What time is your flight back to Catania?'

She stood up to straighten her skirt. 'At 11.30 this evening. Heathrow Terminal 3.'

'I'll have Roland take you out there.'

'Believe me, Aamir, I would stay longer - especially to see your memorial plaque for dear Alice – but my mother is now so very, very frail.'

He gave a knowing half-smile. 'I quite understand.'

While Mrs Kashani busied herself going through her daughter's wardrobe and dressing table drawers, her husband rang his chauffeur on his mobile phone, instructing him to park in front of the tower. After about 10 minutes his wife returned, carrying a small blue rucksack into which she had packed a number of the girl's clothes and a photo album. Tucked under her arm was a small embroidered pillow.

Half an hour later, Reception buzzed on the intercom to say that Kashani's car had arrived. They stood up and moved into the hallway. On a side table, the woman spotted a bulky holiday brochure, with a cover picture showing a sunlit seaside resort. 'Thinking of taking a holiday, Aamir? You never liked holidays, even when Alice was little.'

He glanced down at the brochure and shrugged. 'I thought I might go to Spain for a few days.'

Buttoning his coat for formality, the man accompanied his wife as far as the lift lobby. They cautiously took their leave of each other, briefly clasping hands. He pecked her on both cheeks. 'Safe journey, my dear. And I hope the food is a little better.'

Clutching her parcels, Marta Kashani stepped into the claustrophobic lift car.

I

Andalusia

July 2009

'BULL! BULL!' Anna screamed, pointing through the rear window of the taxi. 'Bull, bull! Look!' Across from the jump seats the children perched on, her father Geoff Evans smiled at his friend Andy Wilmot, as if to say 'We're not going to be fooled by a trick like that!'

Anna persisted. 'Bull! Bull!' Her voice rose above the Spanish football commentary on the car's radio. The driver turned and grinned at the adults. 'Not much further, *Señors y Señoras*.' Andy exchanged a rueful smile with his wife Doreen, seated beside Geoff's petite wife Diane. 'That's the third time he's said that since we left Malaga Airport,' she murmured with irritation.

The limousine had left the metalled autoroute and was now on a dusty track, looping around and passing through the narrowest of concrete underpasses. Now the girls were screaming in unison at a volume Geoff could scarcely believe possible, given that they were only six years old.

Anna was blonde and wore a short blue pleated skirt and a white T-shirt. Her hair had a feathered fringe and her face was freckled. Auburn-haired Lucy wore blue jeans, with her red T-shirt carrying an image of Noddy on its front.

The girls kept pointing through the back window. It was Andy who weakened first, turning to see what they were getting so excited about. Sure enough, framed by the dust the Merc was

1

kicking up, he saw the black silhouette of a huge Miura fighting bull standing proudly on a hilltop. It was all of six metres high. Andy turned back and smiled. 'It's just an advertisement, girls. It's known as the Osborne Bull.'

'Why a bull?' enquired Anna.

'Because they breed especially big bulls in this region.' He thought it best not to explain why.

'So what's it advertising?'

'Brandy,' said Geoff. 'They're just giant steel cut-outs, held up by scaffold poles.'

'Why?' the girls asked in unison.

'So they don't get blown down by strong winds.' The two girls pulled faces at each other, expressing their bafflement.

Parched uncultivated fields lined the track. There was precious little in this arid landscape for horticulturist Geoff Evans to admire. But then, up ahead, the group glimpsed the azure Mediterranean, twinkling invitingly. The two girls screamed with delight at their first sighting of the sea.

The taxi started to slow to a crawl as it approached the arched gateway of a modern holiday complex, above which was a tiled sign reading: LA COVETA PERLA. The arch was roofed with traditional terracotta tiles and flanked by a pair of stately palms. Blue-painted Andalusian tiles decorated the white gateposts. Up ahead, the passengers could make out the stark-white stuccoed profiles of two- and three-storey accommodation blocks. More palm trees flanked the main entrance, with its glass doors swung open.

Geoff and Diane Evans alighted on one side, with their daughter Anna holding her mother's hand. Geoff was in his early-forties. His outdoor work as a self-employed landscape gardener had given his face a healthy tan, which was complemented by his trim haircut. His holiday travel gear of jeans and T-shirt was casual but tasteful.

His wife was a few years younger than him. She was wearing a white tennis skirt, silver trainers and a peacock-blue T-shirt.

Doreen Wilmot took Lucy inside the entrance hall to pick up a luggage trolley. Her husband unloaded their bags from the boot and tipped the driver, who handed him a card. 'Just give me a call any time you want to make a trip into Malaga, *Señor.*'

Geoff swiftly dealt with the signing-in formalities, handing the Wilmots their apartment key. 'We're all on the ground floor. You're in the far corner nearest the pitch-and-putt course. We're over the other side, next to the pool. What say we do a swift unpack and meet up by the pool? Then if they want to' - he looked enquiringly at Anna and Lucy — we could take you girls down to the beach, while your mums unpack.' There were squeals of delight from the youngsters at this suggestion. Turning to Andy he added: 'There's bound to be a beach bar down there.'

While he waited for the two girls to reappear in their beach outfits, Andy strolled around the resort's extensive public areas. He was a few years older than Geoff but their friendship went back to their university days. The two men had hit on the idea of a week's holiday in Spain as both their wives had recently celebrated 'significant' birthdays. It was also Andy's long summer holiday from his teaching job.

Most of the hotel's interiors which he began to explore were in a pastiche of traditional Moorish style. Handsome woven rugs on the walls were interspersed with old bullfight posters. Adjoining a cavernous breakfast room was a long bar, fronted by a tiled dance floor, then a TV room and a library, with newspapers and periodicals in several languages. This overlooked the principal feature of the complex: the Aphrodite Terrace restaurant, shaded by orange trees. Waiters were already laying tables for lunch beside the pool. In the bar, Spanish television was broadcasting the final moments of Andy Roddick's defeat by Roger Federer in the Mens' Final at Wimbledon.

Standing beneath a fig tree outside their apartment, Andy felt Lucy's hand slide into his. He looked down to see that she had changed into a turquoise swim top, worn over a pink mini-skirt and trainers. Anna sauntered up, wearing a similar ensemble in shades of green, with a dark green spotted bandana wrapped jauntily around her forehead.

'OK. So, are we ready to explore the beach, ladies?' Holding hands, the girls excitedly scampered towards the long flight of stone steps which descended to a small cove. Geoff Evans brought up the rear, pausing every now and then to admire the densely-planted verges lining the path, to take pictures on his mobile phone. Great purple clouds of flowering bougainvillaea had shed their flowers, like confetti, onto the steps.

Only a handful of holidaymakers had ventured down to the cove, where a small horseshoe-shaped shingle beach contained a dozen or so of the hotel's blue and white sun beds and umbrellas. A waiter was opening the shutters of a tiny beach bar. The two youngsters surveyed the scene with disappointment. 'BORE-RING - no sand!' fumed Anna, hands on hips.

Ever the pacifier, Andy suggested: 'Never mind, girls. We can still paddle. It doesn't look too deep, does it? Maybe go round the rocks to that cave?' He and Geoff slipped off their trainers and rolled up their trousers, ready to paddle in single file around the edge of the cove. 'You never know there might be pirates' treasure hidden in that cave!' Andy called out as he led the way.

An hour later, the quartet – exhausted but without piratical bounty - wearily climbed back up the steps, eager to sample lunch on the Aphrodite Terrace. A dark-haired gardener, dressed in red overalls, was collecting the fallen bougainvillea flowers in a bucket.

~ ~ ~ ~ ~

The related themes of caves and pirates' treasure were to become regular subjects of conversation on the week's holiday, embroidered by the vivid imagination of the two youngsters. On one of their visits down to the cove, Anna even fancied she could make out the outline of the mast of the pirates' sunken galleon lying on the sea bed. Andy used the missing treasure as the theme for one of Lucy's bedtime stories.

At breakfast on the terrace the next morning, Andy Wilmot found Lucy and Anna avidly reading from two laminated cards headed "*The Legend of La Coveta Perla*". 'The lady at Reception gave these to Anna,' Lucy explained to her father.

'It tells you all about the missing pearls which the pirates hid in that cave we paddled to yesterday' said Anna. 'So it must be true!'

Andy leaned back contentedly in his chair, breaking off from studying the breakfast menu. 'There you are – what did I tell you? That's why this place is called *La Coveta Perla* – the Pearl Cove.'

'So what's a legend?' the ever-curious Anna asked, studying her card.

Andy pulled a face at his friend. 'Erm, it's a sort of story that might or might not be true.'

'Like a fib?' suggested Lucy.

Andy smiled. 'No, I'd say more like one of your fairy stories.'.

~ ~ ~ ~ ~

With the exception of their hearty early morning hotel breakfasts (which the group's resident restaurant critic Anna had pronounced far superior to Weetabix or Corn Flakes) and long nights of blissful sleep, the two girls devoted all their time to the search for La Coveta's missing pirates' pearls. They scoured the seashore at low tide; they studied countless rock pools; and once even ventured nervously into the giant cave itself. They would often be headed for the beach well before 9 a.m. Few other residents were about at that hour, and usually the only person they would encounter on the hundred-plus steps down to the cove, would be the hotel's taciturn gardener, watering the flower beds or sweeping the leaves.

While Andy and Geoff had soon mastered the finer points of the pitch-and-putt golf course, their wives were content to sunbathe by the pool or read English language paperbacks from the library. Each day the two girls would be up well before their parents, decked out in colourful beach clothes and ready to go down to the cove. Inventive Anna's pirate legends grew ever-more unbelievable.

On their third day, seated at their usual breakfast table under an orange tree by the pool, the two girls were attempting to master the rules of a set of dominoes which Lucy had found in the library. One of the young waiters approached them. '*Buenos dias. Qué quierren, señoritas?*'

Lucy gave Anna a mischievous nod and smiled demurely at the man. '*Por favor.*' He took out his order pad and addressed Lucy. '*Por la señorita?*'

'Two boiled eggs with brown bread and butter, please.'

He turned to Anna. '*Y por usted?*'

Without even consulting the menu, Anna announced: 'Waffle with maple syrup and whipped cream, *por favor.*' Lucy was stunned with admiration.

One morning after breakfast, Doreen Wilmot was sitting on the terrace with Lucy, waiting for Anna and her mother so that the four could go down to the cove. Andy and Geoff were at Reception, making a booking for a jet-ski induction session.

Lucy looked up from her Noddy adventure book and pointed at her mother's necklace intently. 'What's that made of?'

Her mother placed one hand across her green necklace. 'My necklace? It's called jade.' A thin line of s-shaped stones formed the design.

'What's jade?'

'It's a semi-precious stone, dear, found in the ground.'

'Where in the ground?'

'I've really no idea. Ask Geoff.'

The waiter who had served them at breakfast approached their table. 'Would Madam like anything to drink?'

'Smoothie!' shouted Lucy without being asked.

'Yes please, Amado. Would you fetch me a *cortado*? And Lucy would like a mango smoothie.'

'Certainly Madam.'

'Do you suppose the pirates hid jade with their pearls and all the treasure?'

'I wouldn't be at all surprised,' her mother said, returning to her novel.

'And who gave that jade necklace to you?'

'Dad. For my special birthday this year.' She placed a hand fondly on the necklace. 'The little green squiggles represent baby fishes. He thought it would make a nice present as my birth sign is Pisces.'

'So what's my birth sign?'

'Leo.'

As Anna and her mother approached, Lucy gave her mother a puzzled expression. 'What's a leo?'

'A lion, dear. It's only a symbol. In fact lots of people think its silly superstitious nonsense, don't they Di?'

'What's that?' Diane Evans pulled up a chair to sit with Doreen.

'Birth signs and horoscopes.' Diane Evans nodded her agreement.

'So what's my birth sign,' Anna asked her mother.

'You're a Taurus.'

'What's a Taurus?'

'It's the sign of the Bull.'

'BULL! BULL!' the two girls gleefully screamed in unison. Then hand in hand they ran off towards the steps down to the cove.

~ ~ ~ ~ ~

The day before the end of their week-long sojourn, Geoff Evans made a solemn announcement at breakfast: 'Well folks, as we're due to go back tomorrow and we haven't even visited the port of Malaga, I propose that we should designate today as Spanish History Thursday. He looked at Andy for support. Do I have a seconder?'

'Durrrghhh. BORING!' was Anna and Lucy's joint response to this announcement.

'Hands up anyone who's heard of the Alcazaba?' Andy asked. Silence greeted the question, which sounded ominously like the start of a history class at school. 'Well Malaga was once the main port serving the Moorish kingdom of Granada and it was guarded by a huge fortified citadel. It is now the largest surviving Moorish fortress in the world. It's more than 600 years old and a World Heritage Site. I really think we should give it a look, seeing it as we're so close. I can easily call Pepe our taxi driver.'

He expected surprise, but the news was greeted with silence, with Anna rolling her eyes skywards. She just wanted to get down to the cove with Lucy. The girls were convinced that they were on the verge of discovering the pirates' lost pearls before the end of the week.

But – as always - it was the adults who had the final word. Within the hour, Pepe was waiting in the front of the complex to ferry them down to Malaga in his Mercedes to explore the world-famous Alcazaba citadel. Lucy and her parents and the Evans stood waiting patiently beside the taxi, for Anna's delayed arrival for the trip into the city. Geoff and his wife exchanged quizzical glances: their daughter was sulking.

But then she appeared from the hotel lobby, sweeping dramatically through the entrance in a pirate's outfit. On her head, over her green bandana, was one of her mother's red scarves, encircled by a bead necklace. The hem of a loose white blouse hung outside her jeans, rolled to three-quarter length and beneath her long scarlet socks she wore black leather shoes, decorated with 'buckles' made from kitchen foil. The whole ensemble was completed with two pheasant's feathers sticking jauntily from her head dress. The adults roared with laughter and Lucy clapped with delight.

Geoff Evans' intended morning of culture was not an unalloyed success, owing to the large number of school groups which had descended on the city's principal historic attraction. It was also intensely hot, with the sunshine radiating off the restored stone fortifications and cobbled paths. A long line of children queuing for ice creams at the tiny cafeteria ruled out any hope of the coffee break the two wives craved. At one point, on their descent, Geoff Evans managed to introduce a novelty which momentarily regained the girls' attention, when he pointed out an ingenious 'double gateway' which the Moors had constructed to deter foreign raiders. It was a dog-legged corridor guarded by two sets of narrow studded wooden gates, four metres tall.

'And what do you suppose they poured down on the enemy from those ramparts up there, after they'd trapped them between these two sets of gates?' he asked.

'Camel poo!' screamed the ever-inventive Anna.

'Dead frogs?' suggested Lucy.

'Nope. Boiling oil.'

'Awesome' was feisty Anna's response as the two girls marched off in search of ice creams, with Anna's Jack Sparrow outfit causing quite a sensation amongst the throngs of Spanish children queuing for ices.

At the final stone archway on the way down towards the exit Andy took a group photo of the friends standing in front Alcazaba's famed Temple Gate. A row of flowering jacaranda trees was perched up high on the ramparts.

Returning to the twenty-first century, the party located their taxi driver, patiently waiting for them under the shade of a clump of palm trees, smoking a cigarette. After Anna and Lucy had finished their ice creams, Pepe suggested taking them all down to the harbour to visit one of Malaga's famous tapas bars.

'So what's "tapas"?' Anna asked Pepe, sitting in the front of the taxi beside the driver. He turned to the grownups for help.

'Salty nibbles,' volunteered Geoff Evans.

'Why salty?'

'To make the customers thirsty and buy more drinks!' Pepe nodded his approval of Geoff's explanation.

Passing through the reception area of the holiday complex a couple of hours later, the English party noted a large *Special Flamenco Evening* poster advertising a live entertainment on the Aphrodite Terrace, featuring a local flamenco dancer, accompanied by a guitarist.

'Can we come too?' the girls asked in unison. 'After all, it is our last night.'

'I'm afraid not, dear.' said Doreen Wilmot. 'You see it doesn't start until 10 p.m. And knowing the Spanish, it will probably go on until one o'clock in the morning. Far too late for you two, especially as we've got an early morning flight home tomorrow. We'll tell you all about it over breakfast and maybe save you some pudding.'

Lucy and Anna put up little resistance as the Malaga sightseeing trip had exhausted them. Their two fathers ordered light suppers for the girls from room service, while their wives attempted to construct something gipsy-like to wear for their terrace dinner.

The four adults were seated at a table by the edge of the pool. Diane was wearing a semi-transparent turquoise evening dress, while Doreen had opted for a pair of red Capri pants and a white silk blouse. The two men (both now sporting decent suntans), wore jeans and T-shirts.

The Aphrodite Terrace was packed to capacity, with the waiting staff all decked out in traditional gypsy costumes. A chubby flamenco dancer – past her prime but still agile with her castanets – entertained the diners, to countless cries of *olé*! But it was her partner's faultless guitar playing – especially with such classics as the serene *Concierto de Aranjuez* – which had the audience spellbound. He stood up, bowed graciously, and indicated that there would be a short interval.

The Flamenco Evening was far from over. At a central table, as the poolside lights were dimmed, four waiters prepared to flambé an elaborate meringue and flan confection. Doreen Wilmot whispered across the table: 'I'll have to miss the firework display. I'm just going to check that Lucy's asleep. All that foot stomping and castanet clacking may have disturbed her.' She quietly rose from the table and headed for their apartment.

To a round of applause and a trumpet fanfare broadcast over the PA system, the waiters ignited the huge pudding. Two of them began busily preparing portions for their colleagues to deliver to the diners.

'ANDY! Come here! NOW! She's GONE!'

The dying embers of the torched pudding momentarily illuminated the grief-stricken face of a terrified Doreen Wilmot, standing in front of the opened door of their corner apartment.

Her husband's dining chair crashed onto the terrace as he dashed towards his distraught wife. He clasped her tightly. 'Come inside, darling. Tell me what's happened.'

Away from the attention of the confused diners, Doreen Wilmot pointed to Lucy's empty bed, with its duvet roughly thrown back. The child's beloved Noddy doll lay on the floor.

'Have you checked all the rooms?'

'Of course I have!' she snapped.

'Bathroom? Loo?'

'Yes, yes, yes.' She began sobbing softly.

'OK. Stay here. I'll fetch Geoff.'

Like a crumpled rag, Lucy's mother sat crying, hunched on the girl's empty bed. Outside, Geoff and Andy conferred in whispers. 'We'd better alert Reception. But discreetly. We don't want to start a hue-and-cry. Not at this hour.'

'Police?' asked Andy.

'Leave that decision to the hotel management. I'd guess they'll want to search the whole complex first. She could have just wandered off half-asleep and got lost somewhere upstairs.' It was a plausible idea which Andy willingly bought into. 'Will you go and tell Diane?'

'Sure. You stay here and look after Doreen.'

All eyes were expectantly trained on Geoff Evans as he returned to his confused wife, sitting alone at their table with an untouched portion of scorched meringue flan in front of her. 'I'm going to tell Reception that Lucy is missing and to ask them to search every room in the place. If we can't locate her, they're going to have to call the police.' Fighting back an urge to burst into tears, Diane nodded. They walked across the terrace towards their room, their arms wrapped tightly around each other.

After a thorough search of every room in the complex – including outhouses, kitchen storage cupboards and even the refrigerators – the duty manager for the night agreed to Andy Wilmot's request to summon the police.

It was well over an hour later that a convoy of police cars slowly approached the complex along the long dirt track. They were mostly white saloons with police markings, all with their blue roof-mounted lights flashing. They pulled up, nose-to-tail, allowing the last vehicle in the convoy – an unmarked black 4x4 – to reverse into 'pole position' in front of the hotel's front door. No one got out.

Several minutes passed, during which time the timid duty manager stood nervously to attention in the entrance porch, ready to officially receive the head of the police delegation. Andy and Geoff stood resolutely behind him, with a handful of nosey guests lingering at the back of the hall. Aural static drifted out into the night from the police cars' opened windows. Sniffer dogs barked excitedly in a police van at the rear of the convoy.

Eventually, the lead 4x4's driver jumped nimbly out and opened the vehicle's back door. A tall blue-uniformed officer stepped out, carefully placed a peaked cap on his head, pulling its polished peak forward and approached the duty manager. '*Señor* Prats? Inspector Holguin from Malaga Guardia Civil. Can we go somewhere to talk privately?' Above their heads there was a ferocious crack of thunder, presaging the approach of a storm.

'But of course, Inspector. May I introduce *Señor* Wilmot – the father of the missing girl – and his friend *Señor* Evans?' No handshakes were exchanged. The Inspector gave a half-nod to the two Englishmen. The nervous under-manager led the group through to his office behind the main reception desk. Heavy rain had already begun pounding the windows.

Holguin (by right of seniority, he'd decided) occupied the manager's seat behind the desk. He removed his cap, setting it down on a leather-bound blotter. He nodded to the other three men to find chairs and sit down. He bristled with arrogance.

Turning to Andy he asked: 'So who discovered the girl's disappearance?'

'My wife Doreen.'

'And she told you?'

'Yes, Inspector.' Andy noted that the appended 'inspector' was well received.

Arms on the desk, Holguin steepled his fingers and closed his eyes. 'And who instituted the search?'

13

After a pregnant pause the duty manager spoke. 'It was I.'

Holguin glared at him. 'Did it not occur to you that valuable forensic evidence – fingerprints, DNA samples – could be jeopardised by such an unauthorised search?'

'No, Sir.'

'We just wanted to find her,' Andy blurted out. 'Forensic evidence was the last thing on our minds.'

Inspector Holguin adjusted the position of his cap on the desk blotter and glanced out of the window as a flash of lightning illuminated the rain-sodden grass on the miniature golf course. 'I see.' Turning to Andy, he asked: 'And tell me, *Señor* Wilmot, were there any discarded items of your daughter's nightclothes in the bedroom?'

'No, nothing. But her Noddy was on the floor.'

'What is this Noddy?'

'It's a famous English toy.'

Inspector Holguin shrugged, reached for his hat and addressed the under-manager. 'The men in the cars outside will now commence a search of the grounds of your complex. Floodlights will be involved. But the incoming storm may hamper our progress. A separate police detachment from Malaga will be deployed at first light to cover the surrounding countryside. Please bring me the girl's passport.' He checked his watch. Looking at Andy and Geoff he added: 'I suggest we meet here again at 6 a.m. And I shall need to check your mobile phones.' It was shortly before 1 a.m. when the conference was concluded.

Doreen Wilmot had retreated to the Evans' apartment on the far side of the terrace and sheltered from the mêlée that surrounded her own rooms. Diane Evans had managed to get Anna back to sleep, though the girl was well aware that something out of the ordinary had occurred. Her mother closed the bedroom door and pulled the curtains to shut out the glare of the arc lights. Doreen sat slumped in an armchair with Lucy's red Noddy doll in her lap.

'Can I get you a hot drink, Doreen?' Lucy's mother shook her head. 'Look, Geoff's already been onto the Foreign Office in London. I dare say they've got a local representative somewhere down this way, so maybe we'll be getting some good news in the morning.'

'The only good news I want to hear is that they've found my Lucy.'

Diane Evans leaned forward in her chair and clasped her friend's hands. 'So do I lovey; so do I.' But there was no response from the other woman.

'At Boots, working in Cosmetics, you get to meet all sorts of people'. Di Evans was trying a fresh tack. 'I sometimes think they come in and ask for something we don't stock just so's they can chat. I've heard that many people's life stories.' Doreen Wilmot's head remained bowed. 'The other day an old biddy came in who'd lost her cat...' The sentence wasn't finished as Doreen had started to sob quietly. Without looking up she mumbled: 'I'm not an old biddy and I certainly haven't lost a CAT !' A brooding silence filled the room.

~ ~ ~ ~ ~

Less than twenty miles away from La Coveta Perla, the rear lights of a black Porsche Cayenne could be seen cautiously proceeding along the litter-strewn track of the huge *Barrio de chabbols* which disfigures the wastelands along the northern perimeter of Malaga Airport. It remains one of the most distasteful social remnants of the post-civil war era.

Downwind from the main take-off runway is a community which will never be featured in the glossy holiday brochures of the Costa del Sol or appear on Spanish Government TV adverts: the Alkabir shanty-town, known to its multi-ethnic residents as Alcatraz. With the daily toxic discharges from the airport's passenger jets and the untreated surface-level sewage, Alcatraz is probably the most polluted township in Spain.

This ramshackle urban hillside community of single-storey shacks, built of breeze-block walls and corrugated tin roofs, houses several hundred urban squatters. Though not as vast as the notorious *favelas* of Rio, Alcatraz is nevertheless a blot on the Andalusian landscape which the Ministry of Tourism would rather not admit exists. Petty crime is rife (murders are not unknown) and few of the town's two thousand plus inhabitants have any formal identification documents. Official police 'culls' are carried out periodically, but more illegal immigrants – usually from North Africa – soon arrive to fill the voids.

After the torrential thunderstorms, the dirt tracks of the shanty town had been turned to mud, liberally laced with the sewage which always runs down the hill. The Cayenne parked at a precarious angle, its headlights pointing up a steep slope with paving steps, picking out a solitary lean-to shack at the top. The driver flashed the main beams then killed the lights. The presence of this opulent foreign vehicle had soon been noted by a gaggle of urchins from the *tugurio*, who quickly encircled it, poised to beg for money as soon as any of its occupants emerged. Their leader – the oldest of the group - wore a face mask, partly to protect his lungs, but principally to establish his credential as *Bandido en Jefe*. Nobody emerged from the black car.

The plywood door of the cottage swung open, sending a shaft of lamplight down the slope. Two figures were silhouetted in the doorway: a tall man in a shabby raincoat clutching a large bundle, and a small female figure in a full burka. The Porsche's lights blinked twice. This was the signal for the couple to descend.

The woman led, illuminating the wet steps with a torch for the man carrying the rug-covered bundle. The couple made their way down the curving flight one cautious step at a time. Their precarious descent took several minutes. Ankle-deep in mud, they stood motionless at the front of the car without speaking. Still none of the three passengers silhouetted inside revealed themselves. The man with the bundle shouted at the hooligans in Arabic to go away but they ignored him.

Minutes later the Porsche's front passenger door swung open and a stocky bald-headed figure, wearing a black leather jacket, gingerly stepped down into the mud, cursing as his shiny black brogues got stained. Then the driver emerged. The light from the car's interior revealed him to be a broad-shouldered East-European with a shaved head. A third passenger remained seated in the back.

Leaving his female companion by the front of the vehicle (now surrounded by begging kids), the tall man carried his bundle to the back of the Porsche. Its rear lights were switched on, showing a small white cross set on a red shield alongside the registration plate. The tailgate slowly rose.

The floor of the large luggage space was covered by a mattress, with a pillow and a folded rug. The man set the bundle down carefully on the bedding and stepped back, grateful to be relieved of the load. The toes of a tiny white foot protruded from one corner of the bundle. The stocky driver covered them with the folded rug.

The tall wraith-like figure, in his wet gabardine raincoat, awaited his reward as the tailgate was lowered. The stout figure in the leather jacket slithered to the back, clutching a large brown jiffy bag. 'No need to count it,' he told the stranger. 'It's all there. Used 50 Euro notes, like we agreed. If I was you, I wouldn't hang about here long.'

The East-European driver returned to his opened door and prepared to climb aboard as the portly paymaster came alongside to give him his final orders. The central console set in the dashboard showed "1:05". 'Barring stops, you should make it in about twenty-four hours, Tomas. Judge your ETA carefully so that you don't arrive too late. The Sisters always retire for the night after *Compline*.'

Without further discourse with the visitors, the shanty-dwellers began their climb back up their front steps, turning halfway to watch the Porsche as it cautiously made its way down the main track leading out of Alcatraz, pursued by the gaggle of shouting urchins.

'So where are they taking her, Omar?'

He shook his head. 'I've no idea, but that vehicle had Swiss plates.'

Metallic pings on their shack roof signalled another downpour.

~ ~ ~ ~ ~

Promptly at 6 o'clock in the morning, Andy Wilmot and Geoff Evans filed into the manager's office. It was still dark outside. Each nursed a strong black coffee. *Señor* Prats shuffled in, dishevelled and none too happy, on account of the complaints he'd been receiving from guests about the use of the floodlights in the grounds during the night. 'The Inspector will be joining us shortly,' he reassured the two Englishmen.

Holguin entered but didn't sit down behind the desk. 'While the search of the grounds is ongoing, I should like to interview *Señor* Wilmot and *Señor* Evans. Please follow me.' He returned the two Englishmen's phones.

As the trio crossed the deserted restaurant terrace Andy realised that the insensitive police inspector was going to conduct his interview in their own apartment. An armed policeman stood at the door.

Within, certain items of Lucy's clothing were being placed in labelled plastic containers by two forensics experts wearing white overalls. Muddy footprints criss-crossed the tiled floor. Holguin moved centre stage. One of the team was slowly wiping small cotton wool dabs in parallel lines across Lucy's pillow. After six parallel passes he placed the pillow in a plastic bag and sealed it with a label.

'*Señor* Wilmot: by which door did you enter this apartment when you heard your wife's call of distress?'

Andy pointed. 'That outside connecting door. The one that leads directly onto the terrace.'

'Was it open or closed?'

Andy thought back to the moment when Doreen had screamed: 'ANDY! Come here! NOW! She's GONE!' He said his wife had been standing outside the room. And that they'd re-entered it by the small door – which was hanging open.

'Open? You're sure?'

'Certain.'

'Did you touch the door handle?' As the inspector uttered the question, one of his specialists slid a plastic bag across the door handle and sealed it with a self-adhesive label.

'I can't be certain, but I don't think so.'

Holguin paced up and down the room. Over the inspector's shoulder, through one of the bedroom's windows, Andy spotted two crouching policemen with powerful torches, studying the ground in the gap in the hedge, connecting the terrace to the pitch-and-putt course. They had covered their heads with waterproof hoods. The policeman briefly watched the procedure then swung round, addressing Geoff Evans. 'And during the whole Flamenco evening did any of your group leave the table at any time?' Geoff shook his head.

'You are quite certain, *Señor* Evans?'

Geoff could see exactly what was being suggested, but stood his ground. 'Positive. Our waiter Amado will confirm that Inspector, I'm certain'.

'I gather you were all due to leave La Coveta later this morning. What time is the flight?'

Geoff Evans answered: 'Eleven o'clock take-off. British Midland to Luton.'

As if issuing a Papal encyclical, the inspector announced: 'Mr and Mrs Evans, with their daughter, may take the flight. But I shall require Mr and Mrs Wilmot to remain at La Coveta.' Turning to the silent under-manager he added: 'Kindly ensure that they are provided with a different room. I am now designating this as a crime scene.' He picked up his hat from the dressing table and strode out.

Andy and Geoff remained seated, dazed by the abrupt and one-sided manner of the interview. Geoff fished his mobile phone from his pocket at the signal and studied the incoming text. 'Good news, mate.'

'I could certainly do with some. What is it?'

'A reply to the text I sent the Foreign Office in London last night.' He scanned the screen and gave Andy an encouraging smile. 'They say they've forwarded it to their Consulate in Malaga and that we should be hearing from a Mr Dominic Martyn. I've given them your mobile number. Right, I think I'd better pop over to tell Di that she can start packing.'

~ ~ ~ ~ ~

There was a light tap on the Evans' apartment door. Diane got up from comforting Doreen and slightly opened the door, half expecting their visitor to be a policeman. 'The Inspector says we can leave this morning.' Geoff Evans whispered, without entering the room. 'Can you start packing? I'll book Pepe for 9 a.m. I need to get back to Andy.' His wife nodded and closed the door.

Diane Evans was reluctant to make too much of a show of gathering their belongings together in front of her distraught friend, who would probably take the news badly, she thought. As she was silently sliding a large case down from the top of the corner wardrobe, the connecting door opened. Anna stood in the doorway in her nightgown, clutching the arm of a teddy bear. 'What's happened to Lucy?' she asked plaintively.

~ ~ ~ ~ ~

The Evans' early morning send-off was subdued and anguished. The two fathers tightly grasped each other's hands, Andy momentarily dropping his forehead onto Geoff's shoulder. 'Text me as soon as you get back, mate?'

'Of course. And you keep us posted. 24/7. OK?'

'Sure.'

Clutching Anna's hand tightly, Diane hugged Doreen. There were too many tears for any words. Mournfully, Pepe closed the boot of the big Mercedes and headed for the airport. At approximately the same hour, eight hundred kilometres away, Lucy was being driven through the gates of the convent of The Sacred Order of the Blessed Sisters of the Immaculate Conception, beside Lake Lucerne.

~ ~ ~ ~ ~

In the hotel's breakfast room all eyes were trained on Doreen and Andy. They picked at their pastries and declined the waiters' offers of cooked food. Andy looked down at his phone as an incoming call was signalled. 'Hello?'

'Good morning. Mr Wilmot?'

'Yes, who's calling?'

'Dominic Martyn. From the British Consulate in Malaga.'

'Good morning, Mr Martyn. Am I pleased to hear from you.'

'I got a message from London during the night. I'm on my way over now. Should be with you within the hour.'

After finishing their breakfast the Wilmots escaped the frenetic activity in the hotel and took refuge on a bench at the old military Battery which looked out to sea.

'I'm going to miss Di. We spent half the night just talking. She was such a calming influence,' Doreen Wilmot reflected.

The couple watched as a dark blue launch, towing a black rubber dinghy, swung into the cove below. POLICÍA was painted on its cabin roof. Two frogmen in wet suits emerged, carrying face masks and flippers and climbed down into the dinghy. They cast it off from the launch and paddled out into the middle of the cove without starting up the outboard motor.

Lying on their stomachs – one at the prow and the other astern – they peered into the water through their masks. This was the first shocking indication to the traumatised couple that the Spanish police believed that their daughter might be dead. On the shoreline of the cove below, about a dozen hotel guests stood silently watching the police operation.

Half an hour later, from their Battery look-out, Andy Wilmot spotted a small black Seat approaching the holiday complex. Leaving his wife on the bench, he strolled down to the car park to meet the visiting diplomat. The young man was no more than thirty years old, well turned out in a lightweight linen suit, a pale blue check shirt and an MCC tie. He was carrying a black leather briefcase emblazoned with the Royal Coat of Arms. Andy led the way into the buildings.

'The library is probably going to be the best place for us to talk, although within the hour I'm expecting a return visit from the Guardia Civil's Inspector Holguin. Shall I get my wife to join us?'

'Not for the present.' They walked across the terrace towards the library. 'So Inspector Holguin is leading the enquiry, is he? I've heard a lot about him down in Malaga, but I've never met him face-to-face. What's he like?'

Having only just met this Government official, Andy Wilmot chose his words carefully. 'Businesslike.'

The diplomat nodded and opened his briefcase and withdrew some files. 'Have they taken a formal statement from you or Mrs Wilmot?'

'No, not yet. The Inspector said that would happen this morning.'

'Well with your permission I think I should be present.'

'I'd welcome it, Mr Martyn.'

'Please call me Dominic.'

'I'm Andy.'

The diplomat was self-assured and efficient – a far cry from the unsympathetic arrogance exhibited by the Spanish police inspector.

'Flights home. I gather that Mr and Mrs Evans have already left?'

'Yes, about an hour ago. Holguin is saying that he wants us to stay on.'

'Quite understandable. I take it that you'd prefer to remain here?'

'I would, but Doreen can't wait to get away. She's still in a dreadful state. Di Evans was an absolute brick last night.'

Martyn crossed his legs and glanced down at the opened file on top of his briefcase. 'Right, I won't beat about the bush. I believe you work with children?'

'That's right. I'm Deputy Head at the Sylvia Pankhurst Academy in Milton Keynes.'

'For how long?'

'Six years now.'

'Now I'm sorry but I have to ask you this Andy: have you ever had any, shall we say, 'administrative problems'. Any complaints made against you? Formal ones that were investigated?'

'What are you getting at, Dominic? The answer, by the way, is an emphatic "no"'.

'We have to cover all bases, Andy. By "we" I mean HMG. And it's best that we get this out in the open and out of the way before your interview, as I can more or less guarantee that as soon as Holguin obtained your passport he would have passed the information onto Interpol in Lyon.'

'To check whether I'm on their sex offenders register?'

'Exactly. So no recorded incidents?'

23

'None at all.'

'How about your relations with parents? After all, you're Deputy Head, so you're probably in the firing line.'

'You can say that again. Mr Wallace…'

'Wallace?'

'The Academy's Headmaster is a Mr Wallace, aka The Wally. Wallace always has "issues" — his jargon for the school's rules and regulations. Things like make-up (a no-no), tattoos (ditto), satchel badges (nothing political), skirt lengths (mid-knee) and footwear (no heels). And hijabs.'

'Did you ever get involved in a dispute with a parent?'

'Yes. But it was minor. Over a hijab. I said it was a hijab and the father claimed it was a purple headscarf. He made a formal complaint. My decision was upheld by the academy governors, but it will be on the record somewhere.'

'No other complaints against you?'

'None'

The discussion was interrupted by the arrival of a young Spanish policewoman, who asked them to accompany her for the interview with Inspector Holguin.

The Spanish police inspector was already seated at the under-manager's desk and rose to greet the British diplomat. The policewoman produced a small tape recorder from her shoulder bag, which she placed in the centre of the desk. Holguin addressed the machine.

'July 17th 2006. La Coveta Perla. Present: Inspector José Holguin; Sergeant Maria Cortez; *Señor* Andrew Wilmot; *Señor* Dominic Martyn of the British Consulate, Malaga.' The policeman leaned forward and pressed the pause button. '*Señor* Wilmot - I propose that my colleague transcribes this session for you to sign. Do I have your agreement?'

Andy looked at the diplomat for confirmation. Martyn nodded.

'Agreed.' The machine was restarted.

The questions were perfunctory, focussing solely on the movements of the two British couples, though Andy Wilmot emphasised that at no time during the entire Flamenco evening did any of the party leave their table. No further details were given about the police discovery during the night of mysterious tyre marks near the pitch-and-putt course, nor whether the forensic examination of Lucy's bedding had thrown any light on her disappearance. The police were clearly holding their cards close to their chests. After about twenty minutes, Holguin switched off the recorder and the policewoman took it away to transcribe Andy Wilmot's statement.

Then the 'bargaining' over the Wilmots' return to Britain began. Doggedly, Dominic Martyn held his own against the intransigent Spanish policeman, with a compromise finally being agreed that the Wilmots were to remain at La Coveta for six more days. Holguin left the two Englishmen to await Andy's statement for signing and shortly after was seen being driven away.

'Not a bad result, Andy, I think you'll agree.' Dominic Martyn took his phone from his pocket. 'I'll get onto the office immediately and have them reserve three seats on next Friday's flight back to Luton.'

'Three?'

'I shall be coming with you. As a precaution.'

'Precaution against what?'

'Press intrusion. Like it or not, Andy, you and your wife are going to be headlines across all the British tabloids. Until Lucy is found. And the first place they'll try to 'doorstep' you will be on the flight home. It's a well-tried technique. So if I'm in the aisle seat – as a sort of 'buffer' - and Mrs Wilmot is sitting by the window, you won't be bothered.'

He cast a wary eye out over the Aphrodite Terrace. 'In fact, I'm rather surprised we haven't had a visit yet from a local 'stringer'.

We'll almost certainly be on all the Spanish news channels tonight. So be on your guard. Luton's another matter, however. The arrival of the distraught parents of an abducted English schoolgirl will have the hacks out in force, I'm afraid.'

'You think so?'

'You'd better believe it. Madonna only has to pop over to Paris to get her toenails painted and there's a scrum waiting for her that would do credit to the Welsh team's front row. London will be putting in a request to the Civil Aviation Authority for permission for you to be picked up on the runway as soon as I've booked our flight. It's highly unorthodox and the CAA are always very difficult about it. Needs must. Who's your MP?'

'Sir Brian Trenchard.'

He took out a smart phone and scrolled down to his *Who's Who in Parliament* app. 'Trenchard you say?'

'That's right.'

'We're in luck – he's a CAA board member – probably because Luton is part of his bailiwick. I'll make sure he gets a FCO message. Right, let's go and take a coffee, shall we?'

'You go on in, Dominic. I'm just going to see how Doreen is. I'll try to get her to join us.'

But Andy Wilmot returned to the coffee lounge without his wife. He shrugged with mild disappointment. 'She's taking a nap. I don't think she got much sleep last night.'

The diplomat collected his papers up and dropped them into his briefcase. 'I must get back to brief the Consul. I'll text you as soon as we get a response from the CAA. If we get the green light, I'll make a similar request to the Spanish aviation authority. Ring me if you have any worries. Anything at all. And do give my best wishes to your wife, won't you?' The two men stood up and shook hands.

An hour later Doreen Wilmot still hadn't made an appearance for lunch. Andy was sitting beneath one of the orange trees when a shadow fell across the Spanish magazine he was reading.

'Mr Wilmot?'

He looked up to see a rather shabby middle-aged man standing in front of him. He wore a black T-shirt under a crumpled beige windcheater, creased brown trousers and scuffed trainers.

'Yes.'

'Stan Murd.' He placed a visiting card on the table in front of Andy. It read: STAN MURD: SPANISH REPRESENTATIVE : EUROPRESS INC.

'Could we have a word?'

'About what?'

'I believe you are the father of the little girl who disappeared from here last night.' Without being invited, the man took a seat at Andy's table. 'Is there anything you can tell me about the police search?'

'I'm afraid that's a question you'd need to address to the Spanish police Mr...' Andy glanced down at the card, which he hadn't touched. '...Murd'.

The unwelcome visitor carried on regardless. 'I'm the Spanish rep for a big European Press conglomerate. We feed Spanish stories to all the English-language papers on the Costas as well as the Press back in England. There are a lot of people who'd like to learn more about how your daughter came to disappear. As well as background stuff about you and your wife.' He produced a small black notebook from his pocket and took out a pencil. 'What do you do for a living, Mr Wilmot?'

Andy could see that the journalist wasn't going to give up. 'I really don't think I can help you Mr Murd.'

'We'd make it worth your while.'

'I'm sorry, I don't follow.'

'If you gave us an exclusive, that is. I'd write it, of course, but you could vet it before I sent it to London. How does that sound?'

'I'm afraid you're barking up the wrong tree.' Andy's dilemma was interrupted by his mobile phone ringing. He glanced at the screen and recognised Dominic Martyn's number. 'Excuse me while I take this call?' He stood up and took a few paces away from the table. 'Yes?'

'Andy? Dominic. I'm on my way back to the Consulate. Good news. In principle, the CAA has approved our request for airside collection for you and your wife. So the office has booked our flights. One or two more diplomatic hoops to get through, but leave that to me.'

'That's excellent. Thank you.'

'Oh and by the way: I gather that flyers with a picture of Lucy are already going up in Malaga; in places like post offices, banks and mini-marts.' As there was no positive response to this news, Martyn asked: 'Everything all right that end?'

Andy glanced across at Stan Murd, who was clearly trying to eaves drop the conversation. 'Err not altogether.'

'I see. Got someone with you?'

'Yes.'

'Like me to call back?'

'Let me just walk over to the Battery, would you? Reception's better up there.' Out of earshot Andy quickly explained his quandary. 'And he's pretty persistent.'

'Stan Murd, you say? That oily creep! You did the right thing, Andy: tell him he needs to contact Inspector Holguin. Nothing more. Got it?'

'Got it.'

'For my part, I'll try to get the Consul here to lodge a formal request for a police guard to be posted at the hotel gates to deter further unwanted intruders.'

'Thank you, Dominic'.

Andy switched his phone off and returned to the table, where Stan Murd was eagerly poised to continue the negotiations. 'I'm sorry Mr Murd, but there's really nothing I can help you with at this stage. I suggest you contact Inspector Holguin of the Spanish police in Malaga.' Slipping his phone in his pocket, Andy got up from the table – without bothering to pick up the journalist's business card - and headed for his new apartment.

Doreen was stretched out asleep, fully clothed, on the bed in their new room. Andy decided it was high time he took some exercise. Even when pounding the side streets of Milton Keynes, jogging always seemed to clear his mind of troubling and extraneous thoughts.

He went down the arid dirt track along which Pepe's taxi had first brought them. That first moment, six days ago, when Lucy and Anna excitedly caught sight of the Mediterranean. Or was it six months ago?

Andy slowed his pace and halted for a breather. Up ahead, midway between where he had stopped and the autoroute, two diagonal coils of dust were spiralling into the sky, accompanied by a dull mechanical drone. It wasn't tractors, as they were moving too quickly across the scrubland. Nor autocross bikes. Their rhythmical movement – almost choreographed – made it seem as if they were searching for something. He jogged closer.

At around fifty metres the puzzle was solved. Uniformed police motorcycle riders, wearing crash helmets, sat astride brightly painted blue and white Quad Bikes, criss-crossing every square metre of waste ground between the motorway and the complex. Occasionally a rider would stop and inspect a hump on the ground. The search for Lucy was certainly thorough. He turned and headed back to the hotel.

Andy decided to take a cooling drink of lager in the hotel bar before going to check whether his wife was awake. There was only one other customer – an elderly gentleman with a white moustache, wearing an un-seasonally thick tweed jacket and corduroy trousers. He was studying the closing London stock market prices in the *Daily Telegraph*.

When his cold beer arrived, Andy nodded at the man, but didn't engage him in conversation. 'Bad business,' mumbled his blimpish neighbour, addressing the mirror at the back of the bar.

Andy took a swig of his lager. 'Indeed.'

'Anything come up?'

'Nothing of any significance so far, I'm afraid.'

'Bad business,' repeated the investor, shaking his head while still avoiding eye contact. He glanced up at the bar clock. 'By Jove is that the time? I promised I'd take the lady wife around the pitch-and-putt.' So saying, he slid off his bar stool and strolled out.

~ ~ ~ ~ ~

On the Friday of their departure, Andy and Doreen walked hand in hand quietly through to the main reception lobby of the complex. All the staff – including Senor Prats – had turned out to bid them farewell, though they were virtually ignored by their fellow guests.

In the car park, Dominic Martyn gave Doreen Wilmot an abbreviated summary of his plan for their journey back to England, omitting any references to the likelihood of Press intrusion on the flight.

'Unfortunately, the Spanish aviation authorities didn't view our request for airside boarding as sympathetically as the CAA. So it will be a bit of scrum at Malaga Airport. Just stay guarded by me and your husband; you'll be seated by the window. And if you need to visit the toilet, just ring the call button and one of the stewardesses will accompany you.

'Now that we've had CAA authorisation, we expect a police car to be waiting for you on the tarmac at Luton. You will be met by a woman Detective Inspector from the Bedfordshire Constabulary – Deborah Tanner – the Senior Investigating Officer who has been assigned to your case. She will be your first point of contact as far as all ongoing enquiries into Lucy's disappearance are concerned.'

'Will we still have to go on dealing with Inspector Holguin?' Andy Wilmot asked.

Dominic Martyn gave a wry smile. 'Fortunately not. Bedfordshire will take care of all cross-authority liaison, intelligence-sharing and keeping you up to date on all developments. Though Malaga continues to lead the investigation, because the crime was committed on Spanish soil.'

'What about you, Mr Martyn – how are you going to get back to Malaga?' asked Doreen Wilmot as they climbed into his car.

'Don't worry about me. I'll probably take a room in one of the hotels at Luton airport, then fly back tomorrow morning. My first duty is to get you both home safe and sound.'

Malaga Airport was even busier than when they had arrived and the Departures Hall was stiflingly hot. After checking in their luggage and passing through the immigration controls, they lined up in a queue for passport checks, flanked by two Spanish policeman. Doreen Wilmot eventually reached the front and slid her opened passport under the screen. Clutching Lucy's Noddy doll close to her body, she looked into the booth at the unsmiling policeman. Fixed to the front of the cubicle's glass screen was an A5-sized poster marked DESAPARECIDA, showing a picture of Lucy. It was the first time she had seen an image of her daughter since her disappearance. She keeled forward as her knees buckled. Only the lightning reaction of Dominic Martyn saved her from crashing onto the marble floor.

At the end of the sky-bridge link between the terminal and the waiting aeroplane, the airline had a selection of free English newspapers for passengers, displayed on a wire stand. Principal amongst these was the UK's biggest-selling tabloid. Superimposed over an aerial view of the *La Coveta Perla* complex was the alliterative headline: 'LITTLE LOST LUCY.'

~ ~ ~ ~ ~

Luton was shrouded in an early-evening gloom as the jet descended, making its final approach to the airport. "We are now approaching Luton Airport London" the cabin tannoy announced, "with our expected time of arrival being seven minutes past six. On behalf of the Captain, I should like to thank you for travelling with Global Airways and trust that you have a safe onward journey."

On landing the trio remained in their seats while the other passengers disembarked. The chief stewardess walked down the empty aisle and nodded to Dominic Martyn, who followed her to the captain's cabin. After several minutes the smiling diplomat returned.

'I think it's going to be OK. The CAA has sanctioned an airside pickup in a police car for you, and a Border Force official will be coming on board shortly to formally inspect your passports. We've been very lucky. I can't see you getting service like this at Heathrow or Gatwick. That sort of red carpet treatment is normally reserved for the likes of Merkle or Sarkozy'

'Not even A-list celebs like the Beckhams or the McCartneys?' Andy asked.

'Nope. They just get escorted through the Arrivals Hall, then they're vetted in private in a hospitality suite.' As he finished, Doreen Wilmot glanced through the window and saw an unmarked people carrier pull to a halt beside the plane's exit staircase. A young policewoman got out of the passenger side, adjusted her black felt hat and stood to attention beside one of the rear passenger doors.

After the cursory inspection of their passports by the Border Force officer, the trio followed the stewardess to the plane's main exit door. The final single-decker bus transporting passengers to the terminal building was moving off just as slanting rain began to fall.

Parked discreetly to the side of the staircase was a black Ford Galaxy, with smoked glass rear windows. The tall slim uniformed policewoman stepped forward and extended a hand. 'Good evening Mr and Mrs Wilmot. Welcome home. I'm Detective Inspector Deborah Tanner, the Senior Investigating Officer who has been assigned to your case.' She glanced at the diplomat standing quietly behind them. 'And you must be Mr Martyn? Thank you for making all the arrangements with the CAA. That was most thoughtful.' The young man nodded graciously. 'Can we drop you anywhere?'

'No, I'm fine thanks inspector.' He nodded towards a large illuminated sign on the side of a tower block beside the runway. 'I'll just head for that hotel.'

Andy shook the man warmly by the hand. 'Thanks for everything, Dominic. I don't think we could have managed it without you.'

'Right, shall we be off?' the policewoman asked. 'I bet you'll both be glad to get home.' She opened a rear door, but Doreen Wilmot just couldn't climb in. In her mind's eye it wasn't a police car but a hearse.

'Come on, Doreen,' her husband gently encouraged. 'Gannin hyem?'

She reluctantly stepped inside. They drove away, waving farewell to Dominic Martyn, carrying his overnight case, heading in the direction of a sign saying IBIS.

The journey was conducted in silence, with the two forlorn parents gazing out of opposite windows at Luton's rain-soaked pavements. Then the car's intercom crackled alive as the detective inspector addressed a colleague.

'Barry? Deborah. How's it looking?'

'Not good.'

'How many are there?'

'About twenty.'

'Jeez!'

'Trouble is, Meadowcroft Way is a cul-de-sac and some of the residents coming home from work can't get into their driveways.'

The policewoman took the phone from her ear and momentarily glanced out of the side window for inspiration. 'Right: get onto the car compound at Newport Pagnell. Tell them to send a tow-truck asap I'll read the riot act to that low life when I get there.'

'Wilco.'

II

Return

_____

MEADOWCROFT WAY, the Wilmot's quiet cul-de-sac on the edge of Milton Keynes, appeared to be unusually busy for a Friday evening. Although all the dozen-or-so bungalows had adequate off-street parking, vehicles were littering the kerbs, some casually parked with their off-side wheels on the pavement. There were saloon cars, 4x4s, a clutch of scooters and at least two large white vans with satellite dishes on the roofs.

'Sorry folks,' the woman inspector called from the front seat. 'It looks as if you've got visitors.'

The police motorcyclist DI Tanner had spoken to on the car radio had parked his bike at the top of the street. Its hazard warning light was flashing, sending blue pulses along the length of the cul-de-sac. The Galaxy's driver slipped through the gap, but had to come to a halt where passage between the two lines of randomly-parked cars was too narrow.

The young officer got out. The headlights picked her up marching smartly to the end of the cul-de-sac, adjusting the brim of her felt hat. As she neared a gaggle of men standing beside the entrance gates of the furthest bungalow, a barrage of flash bulbs went off.

Deborah Tanner walked up to the tallest bystander, who wore a crumpled anorak with a large photographic bag slung over his shoulder. 'Is that your vehicle back there, sir, illegally parked on the pavement?'

'No inspector. I came by cab.'

'Then I suggest you leave the same way — unless, of course, you want to get done for obstruction.' She gestured a thumb over her shoulder aggressively. 'On your way, sunshine!'

She stood on the kerb edge and addressed the throng. 'Move along, there's nothing to see here. A police tow truck is on its way – and I can tell you that as well as the £150 reclaim fine (the Pound does NOT accept credit cards, gents), you'll be going all the way to Bedford to pick up your cars and vans.'

There was no immediate mass movement from the assembled journalists and photographers, though a handful began to slink off in a desultory fashion, mumbling sexist insults. To no-one in particular, Deborah Tanner observed in a stage whisper: 'Grub Street's finest. Don't they just love to hunt in a pack?'

She took out her pocket book and folded back its cover. 'Right. Sixty seconds. Then I'm going to start collecting names and addresses to bring charges of wilful obstruction.' The exodus got bigger and within 10 minutes – save for the discarded polystyrene coffee mugs, cola cans and empty cigarette packets on the pavement – some semblance of normality had returned to Meadowcroft Way. The curtain-twitching neighbours went back to their TVs.

The driver pulled the police vehicle into the front drive of the furthest bungalow and Doreen and Andy got out. Leaving her driver to stand guard at the front door, the inspector followed the couple inside. As she stepped into the Wilmot's kitchen the young woman removed her hat to reveal a striking platinum-tinted buzz cut hair style.

While Doreen boiled a kettle for coffees, Andy and Deborah sat at the kitchen table. 'I'm sorry to tell you folks that you're going to get a lot more of that sort of thing. They'll get even more cunning and devious, trailing you around the shops; even whispering offers of huge sums of money for exclusives. So plan your trips outside with care. And speak to no-one.'

She placed a visiting card on the table. 'Put this on the kitchen notice board over there. I'm your first point of contact. Your ONLY point of contact. You're to keep me up to speed on ALL your movements. For my part, I'll keep you posted about all the developments in Andalusia. I promise.' The forthright way in which this young woman spoke impressed the Wilmots. Doreen placed coffee mugs in front of them and opened a biscuit tin

'Mrs Wilmot: when do you have to return to work? I understand you are a dental receptionist.'

'Monday morning.'

'Think you can manage it?'

'I doubt it'

'OK. Ring your doctor for a sick note and phone in to the dental surgery first thing on Monday morning. Say you'll be off for several days. Mr Wilmot — you're a schoolteacher I believe. Deputy Head at the Sylvia Pankhurst Academy, isn't it?'

'That's correct, inspector.'

'When do the summer holidays end?'

'Pupils are back a week next Monday. But I'm due to go in on the Friday before. Timetables and staff rosters — that sort of thing.'

'Are you OK with that?'

'Sure. I'd rather be doing something than sitting here waiting for the phone to ring.'

'That's the spirit. Listen folks, we're going to win this one, believe me. And just remember who said it, the night you arrived home.'

Staring blankly into her coffee mug, Doreen Wilmot began to sob quietly. She excused herself from the table, mumbling something about unpacking, and left the room. DI Tanner stared down at her empty mug. 'Me and my big mouth.'

For his part, Andy told the feisty policewoman about the statement he'd had to sign before leaving Spain and about Inspector Holguin's request for a photo of Lucy.

'Did he ask to see your mobile phone?'

'Yes. Mine and Geoff's', but he returned them within the hour.'

'I expect he was only checking the calls you'd made around the time of Lucy's disappearance. So tell me – on the holiday, who was it who took most of the photos?'

'Geoff and me mostly. My wife's not really a techie. Geoff took loads – mainly of trees and plants; he's a landscape gardener.'

'The girls?'

Andy chuckled. 'They were too busy looking for buried treasure. I suppose you could say I was the party's official photographer for all the group shots.'

'Mind if I have a look at them?'

'By all means.' Andy took the phone from his pocket and slid it across the table.

'Thank you. Did you by any chance take any shots at the Flamenco evening?'

'I'm afraid not.'

'Pity'. She popped the phone into her bag. 'I'll drop it in on Monday after we've copied anything relevant, if that's OK.' She stood up. 'I expect you two will want to have an early night, so I'll be making tracks. And remember what I said about the hacks.'

'I will. Thanks inspector. We're both extremely grateful. Sorry about Doreen crying just now. She's taking it very badly.'

'I'm sure I'd be the same if I had kids.'

He followed her to the door and watched the rear lights of the Galaxy as it drove away up the deserted cul-de-sac, followed by the motorcycle.

III

Norfolk News

IT WAS NOW eight days since Lucy's disappearance. The Wilmot's first Sunday back in Meadowcroft Way was a sombre and subdued affair. Doreen Wilmot didn't emerge until well after 11 o'clock, as her husband was compiling a shopping list to replenish the bare pantry and refrigerator. He switched the kettle on to make a fresh pot of tea as his wife slumped down at the kitchen table. Placing a hand on her shoulder he asked: 'Sleep OK?'

She shook her head wearily. 'Not really. I got up in the night and took a couple of sleeping tablets. They seemed to do the trick. But I feel terrible right now.'

He completed the brew and handed her a mug. 'Well take this back to bed. I'm going to drive over to Waitrose to do a major re-stock. What do you fancy for Sunday lunch, Doreen?'

She stared at the mug of tea but didn't look up. 'I'm not bothered. You choose.'

Trying unsuccessfully to lighten his partner's mood, Andy said: 'Right, leave it to me. It'll be a surprise. And I'll cook it.' Without responding, Doreen Wilmot got up from the table and slouched back to their bedroom.

Andy had completed his shopping list and was collecting three dark green cold bags from the pantry, when the house phone rang. He half-expected it to be Geoff Evans, but the screen showed a number he didn't recognise. He picked the phone up. 'Hello?'

'Mr Wilmot? Deborah. Deborah Tanner.'

'Good morning, inspector. Working on a Sunday?'

'Sort of. I'm at home, but I've just had a message from Kempston. Our duty sergeant took a call from someone in Norfolk earlier. It looks as if we may have a major break-through. But I wanted to check it out with you first. Have you got a minute?'

'Sure. I was only going to go to the supermarket.'

'How's your wife?'

'In bed.'

'I see. OK – here's the situation. Do you remember meeting a fellow Brit when you were staying at *La Coveta Perla* named Mark Wareing?'

'I don't think so.'

'Only he says he spoke to you in the bar one night. About football?'

'Sorry, I don't recall him. You say he's phoned in to police headquarters? Why so?'

'Long story, but I'll keep it brief. It seems he and his wife had a first floor apartment facing yours across the terrace at the back. But they checked out and flew back to England on the morning that Lucy disappeared in the night. So they wouldn't have been interviewed by the Spanish police.'

'Sorry, Inspector, I'm not with you.'

'No, it's me. I'm just a bit – well, excited about it; I think it might be a significant development. According to Mr Wareing, he was out on his balcony early one morning having a cigarette before his wife got up, when he noticed some suspicious activity in the vicinity of your apartment.'

'What sort of suspicious activity?'

'A tall man in red overalls was peering through your apartment window. The witness says he thinks he's the gardener on the complex; he remembers seeing him cutting the grass on the pitch-and-putt course.'

Andy Wilmot was momentarily lost for words. 'You still there?'

'Yes. Just trying to take it all in. I remember the gardener. Bit of a facer, isn't it?'

'I'd say.'

'Did you say this witness lives in Norfolk?'

'Yes. He works in a food factory outside Thetford. I told him I'd like to take a statement from him. I'll have to square it with Norfolk, of course, as it's their patch. I was wondering – it's a bit of a cheek – but how do you feel about doing a sketch plan of the hotel complex for me to take to the interview? Being a Sunday, there's no one here I can ask to do it.'

'Yes, inspector, I'd be happy to. Lucy's really the artist in this house...' He let the sentence tail away, realising its futility.

'You're a star! Call me Deborah or Debs, by the way, but NOT Debbie please!'

'I'm Andy.'

'You're a star, Andy. How would it be if I picked it up in the morning? Say about eleven. Then I'll head on up to Thetford.'

'Right you are. I'll see you tomorrow.'

After checking that his wife was asleep, Andy Wilmot reversed their Mini Cooper from the garage and headed for the city centre. The supermarket car park was already three-quarters full.

But it wasn't the sight of the busy aisles or the long queues at the checkouts which deterred him. It was the headlines on every one of the Sunday newspapers on the supermarket's newsstand facing the entrance doors. Most showed night-time shots of Meadowcroft Way, with the Wilmots walking up their front path; two had aerial pictures of their Spanish holiday complex; while one had a grainy picture taken at their wedding. The attention-grabbing headlines were just as upsetting for Andy: 'SAD HOMECOMING' and 'LOST LUCY'S PARENTS' SAD RETURN' were the most gut-wrenching. Andy felt utterly sick and wanted to turn around and go home. But a gentle tug on the sleeve of his jacket stopped him from moving away.

'Mr Wilmot?'

He looked down at a dark-skinned boy of 8 or 9, dressed in casual clothes, with a skateboard tucked under his arm. 'Hello Randolph. Ready for school next week?'

The boy was suddenly tongue-tied in the presence of the Deputy Headmaster. 'I suppose so, Sir - though I still haven't finished the holiday project you set us.'

'That's OK Randolph – there's still a week to go.' He was aware that a plump West Indian woman was watching them from the vegetable aisle. She gave Andy a knowing nod and smiled, but didn't approach.

'It's just – Mum's says she's so sorry to hear about your daughter. She says to tell you she hopes they find her very soon.'

Andy fought resolutely to control his emotions. This was the closest he'd come to breaking down. He'd weathered his daughter's disappearance on the Flamenco night; put up with the self-important Spanish inspector; managed to bid farewell to Geoff and Diane without piping an eye; and taken comfort from the admirable diplomat, Dominic Martyn. Now faced with the plaintive look of a small schoolboy, he just wanted to burst into tears and hug him. Instead, what came out was controlled but courteous. He nodded slowly at Randolph. 'Yes and so do I. Tell Mum thanks, will you Randolph? I really appreciate it.' He waved to the boy's mother.

~ ~ ~ ~ ~

The following morning, Andy was putting the finishing touches to a very competent A3 sketch plan of the Spanish holiday complex, when he heard a car pull up outside. He had left Doreen asleep, with her morning tea cold and untouched. He managed to get to the front door before Deborah Tanner set off the door chimes.

The Detective Inspector looked trim and professional and gave him a nice smile. She was wearing a crisp white blouse under her dark blue jacket, above a blue pencil skirt. 'Good morning, Andy. Here, I've brought your phone back.' She handed him his iPhone.

They walked silently into the kitchen and closed the door. She removed her hat, with its distinctive blue-and-white checkerboard hat band, and placed it on the table. 'The prints should be ready when I get back from Norfolk.' Bending forward to study the detail of his drawing, she observed: 'That's pretty impressive, if I may say so.'

'Thank you. I taught art before I became Deputy Head.'

'I'd like to use it back in our Major Incident Room at Kempston, if that's OK? After I've shown it to Mark Wareing today.'

'Of course.' The kitchen clock showed 11.10.

'How's your wife?'

He made a fluttering motion with one hand. 'So, so. Her sister's going to pop round at lunchtime and I've cleared everything with the surgery. So what's this place you're visiting in Norfolk?'

'Apparently it's a chutney factory. Italian-owned.' She glanced at her notebook. 'Tillington Foods. The fellow I'm going to see is their Goods-In Manager. So you don't recall chatting to him?'

'I'm afraid not.'

'No worries.'

She picked up her hat. 'I'd better make tracks. If I have anything positive to report after the interview, I'll give you a call. Oh, and could you give me Mr Evans' phone number? I ought to get him to check through his pictures too.' Andy rolled up the sketch plan and wrote out Geoff's mobile number.

~ ~ ~ ~ ~

It was just before 1 p.m. when the policewoman's unmarked Vauxhall Astra pulled into Tillington Foods' car park. The last unit in a cluster of food-related factories, the company's plant comprised two long single-storey wings set on either side of a three-storey central office block, on the top of which – at a rakish angle – was a giant chutney jar labelled 'ECCO'. The pungent smell of vinegar and beetroot was everywhere.

The door of a black Ford Fiesta swung open two bays away from the Astra and a young black policewoman, carrying a shoulder bag, got out. She walked across to greet the senior officer. 'Detective Inspector Tanner? Good morning, I'm WPC Proctor; assigned to your case to tape your interview with Mr Mark Wareing.'

'Good to meet you, constable. Let's go inside, shall we?'

The inspector announced herself efficiently to the woman receptionist, handing her a card. A few minutes later Mark Wareing appeared from a rear door linked to the factory. He wore yellow ankle-length rubber boots, a white overall coat and a white mesh hairnet. After formal greetings, the trio moved to a small windowed alcove with a side table in the corner of the reception area.

'Would you rather go somewhere more private, inspector? I can soon fix a conference room for us.'

'Here's fine so long as you're happy?'

'Fine by me.'

Deborah Tanner unrolled Andy Wilmot's sketch and held it flat on the table with her driving gloves, while the young police constable set up the tape recorder. 'I brought this along so that you might explain the layout of the complex.'

'Good idea.'

'Before we start, may I just ask why it was a week since your departure from La Coveta Perla that you contacted Bedfordshire Constabulary?'

'The day following our return from Spain I had to go on a week-long DEFRA course on food hygiene in Liverpool, which the firm had arranged for me to attend. To tell you the truth, inspector, they worked us so hard I didn't see a newspaper all week. It was only after seeing all those lurid stories in yesterday's Sundays that the penny dropped.'

'That's a fair enough explanation.' Deborah Tanner nodded to the young policewoman, who switched on the recorder. 'Right, Mr Wareing: in your own words.'

The manager paused, then began to recount the strange early morning sighting he had witnessed. 'It was our last day at La Coveta – so that would make it the Thursday. First thing – usually around six – I liked to go out on the balcony for a ciggie, as my wife can't stand smoking indoors. I'd sit on a chair and just enjoy the early-morning atmosphere - before the sun came up and it started getting hot. There was never anyone around at that hour. Even the waiters didn't start laying up the tables for breakfast until around 6.30 a.m.

'Anyhow, after about ten minutes – so that would make it about 6.10 or 6.15 – I saw a figure in a one-piece red overall, like the Ferrari mechanics all wear in Formula 1. He emerged from the gap in the hedge that connects the terrace with the golf course.'

'Can you describe what else this man was wearing?'

'Bright yellow leather gardening gauntlets and black rubber boots. And he was carrying a yellow-handled strimmer. Holding it midway by the drive shaft, parallel to the ground'

'And you say he'd appeared from the direction of the pitch-and-putt course?'

'That's correct. I naturally assumed he'd been doing a bit of early morning maintenance – though now I come to think of it, I hadn't heard the strimmer going. You can't easily mistake the sound of a grass strimmer!'

'Was he wearing a protective helmet or goggles?'

'No, he was bare-headed. He had a thick head of black curly hair. He was dark-skinned; I'd say Algerian or Moroccan. He paused in the opening, set his strimmer down on the paving and moved cautiously towards the corner of the building.'

'Can you show us on the plan please, Mr Wareing?'

The food factory supervisor indicated a corner of the building shown on Andy Wilmot's sketch. Deborah nodded to WPC Proctor to pause the recording. 'As this is oral only, Mr Wareing, can you describe what you're pointing out on the sketch plan?'

'Certainly inspector.' The machine was re-started.

'I saw the gardener approach the corner of the ground-floor apartment closest to the entrance to the hotel's pitch-and-putt course.' Deborah nodded her approval of the description. 'Just to the right – and partially shaded by a big fig tree - there was an outside door onto the terrace. The gardener looked through the window, shielding it with his gloved hands as if trying to see what was inside. Then he moved around the side, out of sight, under the fig tree.'

'So you can't be certain if he actually checked to see whether the side door to the apartment was locked or not?'

'No.'

'How long was he lost from your sight?'

'Two or three minutes at the most.'

'And then?'

'He reappeared. Walked quickly across the terrace, picked up the strimmer and disappeared onto the golf course through a gap in the hedge. About five minutes later I heard the machine in action.'

'I don't suppose you took any pictures on your phone did you?'

'I'm afraid not inspector, though it was on the table beside my ciggies. At the time, I just put the whole thing down to one of the hotel staff being a bit nosey. It was only when I saw the Sunday papers that I realised it might have more significance.'

'Of course. Well thank you very much, Mr Wareing.' She nodded to her colleague to end the recording. 'What I propose – with your agreement – is that the constable here returns to Norwich to transcribe your statement, which she will bring back tomorrow for you to sign. Obviously I'll be sent a copy electronically.'

'Perfectly OK with me, inspector.' They shook hands and the manager returned to his warehouse.

~ ~ ~ ~ ~

Within less than two hours of her arrival at the chutney factory, Deborah Tanner was making her way back down the A14 carriageway, towards the busy Cambridge by-pass. She felt quite elated. She reset her satellite navigation, switched her phone to speaker mode and put in a call to her assistant, Wendy Owen, at Bedfordshire Constabulary's headquarters.

'Hi Debs! So how did it go?'

'All good stuff. Very level-headed and thoughtfully presented. You can see why that bloke's a manager. Norwich is handling the transcription and they should be sending a copy across for me later this afternoon. Wareing has confirmed that he saw a hotel staff member peering into the Wilmot's apartment early one morning.'

'Wow. So what's the next step?'

'Good question. Well, obviously we can't keep this to ourselves. We're going to have to share it with Malaga. I'll ring Mr Wilmot and tell him. Heaven knows what Holguin will do with it. If the roles were reversed and it was up to me, I'd have that staff man in for questioning like a shot. AND I'd keep him in for the full ninety-six hours.'

'Do you think that's how Holguin will play it?'

'Search me. That bloke's an enigma.' She drove past a sprawling hi-tech business park on the outskirts of Cambridge which dwarfed little Tillington Foods' Thetford operation.

After a short silence, Deborah added: 'It's my belief that this was no opportunist crime, Wendy, though such things do happen. My gut reaction tells me that this was a meticulously planned operation. Mark Wareing has as good as confirmed that somebody was casing the Wilmot's apartment just sixteen hours before the girl disappeared. Have you got any news for me yet about those phone pictures?'

'Not so far, Debs. I'll chase the lab again. By the way, a new member joined the MIR team this afternoon: HOLMES has arrived!

'Wow! Tell me more.'

'It's simply awesome the things it'll do. All in a split second.'

'Such as?'

'The bloke you interviewed today – Mark Wareing.'

'What about him?'

'I checked to see if he had any previous. He's got two speeding offences recorded on his licence and last month he had to attend a Speed Awareness course in Norwich.'

'See, babes – I told you it was a neat piece of kit.'

'Did you put in a call to Holguin?'

'Of course I did. As soon as I left the factory. But it was on voicemail.'

'He was off playing golf.'

'How on earth do you know that?'

'Ah hah. Not much gets past little Wendy! By the way, you know you asked me to book you a slot tomorrow with the chief? Well his secretary says he's going to be tied up all day.'

'Doing what?' snapped Deborah.

The inspector's secretary gave a hoot of laughter. 'Apparently he's seeing a delegation from Clarence House. And they want lunching. It's about the supermarket opening next Saturday. Surely you haven't forgotten, Debs: Camilla's coming to MK!'

After chatting with her secretary, Deborah Tanner called Andy and gave him a quick summary of Mark Wareing's early-morning 'sighting', being careful not to give too many details. 'I'm hoping the pictures from your phone will be finished tonight. If there's anything on them, I might drop them round in the morning, if that's OK.'

'Sure'.

'Now I'm just going to call your friend Geoff, in case he's got any images on his phone that we ought to take a look at. I'll call you tomorrow.'

Deborah reached Geoff Evans just as she was crossing back into Bedfordshire. 'Mr Evans? I'm Detective Inspector Tanner of Bedfordshire Constabulary. I'm the Senior Investigating Officer assigned to work with Andy and Doreen Wilmot.'

'How can I assist you, inspector?'

'Mr Wilmot tells me you took quite a lot of pictures on your phone when you were on holiday together. It's any that you might have taken in the hotel grounds that I'm interested in. I gather you're a horticulturalist.'

'That's right. I'm a landscape gardener. The hotel's grounds were exceptionally well-planted. Some amazing bougainvilleas in full flower. Stunning displays.'

'Did you take any pictures of them?'

'Lots.'

'Right, now listen carefully. Could you go through them for me and see whether any of them show a gardener in the background? He'll probably be wearing a one-piece red overall. And he's got a shock of black hair. Got that?'

'Yup. Give me a few minutes and I'll call you back.'

'I'm most grateful, Mr Evans.'

'And how's poor Doreen? She was pretty low when we left.'

'Not much improvement, I'm afraid. She's still off work.'

'Tell her Di sends her love?'

'I certainly will.'

Geoff Evans got back to the police officer within a quarter of an hour. 'Sorry it took so long. There were hundreds of them though only about a dozen of the flower beds beside the steps leading down to the cove.'

'Any with a gardener in?'

'Two. Red overalls like you said. In one he's got his back to the camera, but the other shows quite a clear profile. Would you like me to ping it across to you?'

'That would be very helpful, Mr Evans.' Deborah Tanner was giving him Wendy Owen's email address just as she drove into Kemspston, the headquarters of Bedfordshire Constabulary.

~ ~ ~ ~ ~

Early on the Tuesday morning – the twelfth day since Lucy's disappearance – Andy Wilmot was nursing a strong mug of coffee, still in his pyjamas. He was trying to get to grips with the timetables and teachers' rosters for the new term. It was shortly after 8 a.m. and though he had taken his wife her first cup of tea, he could hear no signs of movement. His mobile phone signalled an incoming call from Deborah.

'Good morning! At work already?'

'Yup, been here since six. What about you?'

'Autumn term timetables. Not the most exciting of exercises.'

'Well needless to say, there's no word yet from Malaga. But if they haven't hauled that Moroccan in for questioning by mid-morning, I'm going to let old Clouseau have it with both barrels.'

'Clouseau?'

'Wendy's new nickname for Inspector Holguin. But the good news – and I was ringing to ask if I could drop round – is what one of our ace lab technicians has done with those holiday snaps on your mobile phone.'

'Tell me more.'

'No. I want you to see them with your own eyes, Andy. I was too quick off the mark yesterday describing Mark Wareing's information as a breakthrough. But this stuff is in a different league. Can I bring them round?'

'Sure. I'm here all morning.'

Just as he ended the call, Andy's wife appeared in the kitchen doorway. Her hair was matted and it looked as if she'd been sleeping in her dressing-gown. 'Was that your lady friend I heard you talking to on the phone?'

'If you mean Detective Inspector Tanner, yes it was. She's got some interesting news, which she's bringing round to show us.'

'How nice.' Doreen Wilmott banged her empty tea mug on the table, turned around and headed back to the bedroom.

~ ~ ~ ~ ~

Deborah Tanner was at the Wilmot's bungalow within the hour, dressed in civilian clothes: a pink blouse, blue jeans and black suede pumps. Andy decided she looked quite glamorous as a private citizen. She had a big grin on her face as she removed a rolled-up set of glossy A3 colour prints from her shoulder bag. She used two empty coffee mugs to hold the thick photographic paper flat on the table.

'Exhibit 1: the British party awaiting the arrival of its luggage in front of a carousel at Malaga Airport's Arrivals Hall, if I'm not mistaken?

'Correct.'

'Exhibit 2: your shot dated 12th July, showing Mr and Mrs Evans, plus Anna and Lucy sat a table, in what looks like the terrace restaurant at La Coveta.'

'Correct again. That was the morning after our arrival. Shortly after this was taken, Geoff and I took the girls down to the cove.'

Deborah pointed a finger above the heads of the seated grown-ups. 'OK. Now look behind your wife and the Evans. See the barman polishing glasses under that sun umbrella?'

'Eh yes. I think he's called Amado.'

'Now look behind his left shoulder? A bit fuzzy and shaded, but it shows a distinctive profile of a stout, bald-headed man. Standing behind him, but looking in your group's direction. Wearing a black jacket. Got him?'

'Yes, I think I can make him out. I've no idea who it was. Could be the under-manager Prats. He's about the same proportions.'

Deborah peeled the terrace picture away to reveal an altogether different image. 'Thursday 15th July, according to the camera date stamp. Three days later. So where was this taken?'

'On our excursion to the fortified Moorish citadel of Alcazaba. Geoff wanted the girls to see it as it's a World Heritage site. This one shows us in front of what they call the Temple Gate.'

'And standing in the gateway we have: Geoff and Diane Evans with Lucy. And on the extreme right of the group, would that be Jack Sparrow?'

Andy chuckled. 'That's Anna. I think it was her way of registering a protest that she and Lucy couldn't go looking for buried treasure down in the cove!'

'Now look through the archway. Who is that standing in the pool of sunshine beside the ice cream shack the children are queuing in front of? Remind you of anyone?'

'So what are you saying, Deborah?'

'It's not what I'm saying, Andy; it's what I'm showing you. Clear evidence that on three occasions you were being stalked. Right from the time you flew into Spain.

'And if you're still in any doubt, may I present Exhibit 4? Hey presto!' She rolled the Alcazaba shot back to reveal the three silhouettes of the unidentified male figure. 'They're identical in every detail. Look: ears, squat chin, square shoulder line and a bald head. Black Jacket for sure.'

'How sinister.'

'I know it's bloody creepy isn't it? To think that he might even have been on your flight. But then this whole affair is becoming pretty creepy. It's unquestionably the same man in all three shots. No doubt about it. I'd stake my police pension on it - and with twenty years' service it's worth quite a bit. Matey's wearing a black jacket and tie in all the pictures. A Spaniard would never be dressed like that in summer. And that dark complexion. What do you think: Moroccan?'

'Possibly. Or Asian. OK I'm convinced. But perhaps he's just a curious onlooker or a peeping tom. Maybe a pervert who likes watching little girls?'

'In three different locations, four days apart? And for all we know there were other places he tailed you that aren't recorded.'

'But how can you prove that this man planned and carried out the abduction of our daughter?'

'I can't. But in the current jargon I'd say we should definitely regard Mr Black Jacket and the gardener in the red overalls as 'persons of interest'. The policewoman jabbed her finger at the silhouettes. 'It's my belief that this man commissioned the crime, and that the gardener – possibly with an accomplice – was the agent. I'm going to have to send these images to Malaga, I suppose, even though they've shared bugger-all with us so far.'

'Why do you suppose that is?'

'You mean their lack of co-operation? Well, for one thing there's Malaga's close proximity to Gibraltar. It still rankles down there. For another thing, back in the 1980s, that part of Andalusia was infested with British criminals, and we did nothing about extraditing them. Surely you remember the scandal? The Press even dubbed it the Costa del Crime. Which didn't go down well with the regional tourism board.'

Deborah's theories were interrupted by the ring of her mobile phone. 'Wendy! Any news from your friend Inspector Clouseau?'

'Yes. He sent two officers out to *La Coveta Perla* this morning to pick up the gardener and take him down to headquarters for questioning.'

She gave Andy a wink. 'Bloody brilliant!'

IV

Force HQ

THE FOLLOWING morning Andy Wilmot was preparing to drive over to his school, to deliver the completed staff rosters for the new term. His wife was having a lie-in after another disturbed night's sleep. It was the thirteenth day since Lucy's disappearance.

His mobile rang just as he was about to head for the garage. He checked the screen and saw that it was Deborah Tanner calling.

'Morning Deborah.'

'Good morning Andy. All OK at your end?'

'Yup, much the same as yesterday. I haven't shown Doreen those blow-ups yet. I think I'm going to have to choose the moment carefully.'

'Wise man. No word from Holguin, I'm afraid. I can't decide if that's good or bad. What do you think?'

'Par for the course, I'd say.'

'Agreed. Apt metaphor too. If they do charge the gardener I hope they'll have the courtesy to ring me straight away. I think I might just email him to that effect. I'd love to pop across to Malaga with Wendy to liven things up a bit, but as it's their show by rights we should wait to be asked.

'Look, I'm sorry to be a pain, but would you have time to call by at Kempston some time today? It's just that I'm stuck here waiting for the chief to see me. I daren't set foot outside the building until I've briefed him.'

'Sure. Be glad to. I was just on my way to school when you rang. So I can easily make a detour and call in on the way there. Or else on the way back. Which would you prefer?'

'Tell you what: why not make your visit after you've been to the school — say oneish? I'd like you to meet one of the team — Dave Williams. We could go and grab a bite in the canteen, though I won't be able to show you our MIR as it's out of bounds to civilians. You might even get to meet the redoubtable Wendy Owen.'

'That sounds good. I know where you are so I'll be along at 1 p.m.'

~ ~ ~ ~ ~

Bedfordshire Constabulary's headquarters turned out to be a solid-looking group of 1970s buildings, set in landscaped grounds. Constructed entirely of a warm red local brick, a long two-storey wing, punctuated by an archway into an inner yard, linked with a three-storey wing which was surmounted by a radio mast. Above the archway was the county's coat of arms.

The security guard at the main door directed Andy to the reception desk, where he was asked to sign in. The receptionist handed him a lanyard marked VISITOR and put in a call to Deborah Tanner. The young police inspector appeared after a couple of minutes. She shook him warmly by the hand.

'Welcome to Kempston.'

'Very smart workplace you've got here, I must say.'

'Yes. It's certainly a cut above most of the force HQs I've seen.'

'How many work here?'

'Police and civilian backup is currently about 300. Let's go into the canteen; it's in the other block. Dave has bagged us a table.'

They walked across the internal courtyard, which was full of neatly-parked police cars, vans and motorcycles.

The canteen was cavernous, hot and extremely busy. Handing him a tray, Deborah shepherded her visitor along the self-service queue and paid for their meals. She led the way to a window table where a man beckoned them cheerily. 'Dave — this is Andy Wilmot, Lucy's father. Andy: meet my No 2, Sergeant Dave Williams.' As they took their seats, Deborah added: 'Dave hails from Gateshead. He's my traffic and transport expert. As well as my private guru.'

The man smiled and in a broad Geordie accent said: 'Pleased to meet you, Andy.'

It wasn't until they were tackling their treacle puddings that Deborah referred to the case for the first time. 'I may get a call at any moment to go and brief the chief upstairs, so it might be useful if we gave Andy a quick update. Do you want to go first, Dave?'

'Sure.' He addressed his remarks to Andy. 'Well, we know that the car used was a Mazda hatchback. Holmes worked that out for us from data Malaga had sent over − tyre widths, rear track measurements etc − after they found tyre marks in the gap in the hedge by your apartment. This morning they emailed us to say that there had been five Mazda hatchbacks reported stolen on the night your daughter disappeared.'

'Sorry to be dense, but who is Holmes?'

Dave Williams smiled. 'HOLMES stands for Home Office Large Major Enquiries System. Developed for the Home Office by one of the big American IT companies. Obviously christened by a British civil servant with a sense of humour. It's been around since the 1980s. Most forces have them now.'

'What does it do?'

'Just about everything - except make the tea. It's a computer-based admin aid, which processes and analyses every scrap of information which we collect. So, for example, while Malaga has been manually cross-checking all your fellow guests at the complex for possible criminal records, our Wendy can get HOLMES to do it in a nano-second.'

'And will Malaga have run all the hotel guests' names through the Interpol register?'

'If they've done their job properly, sure. Staff and guests.'

'Even me?'

'You better believe it, man. You'd have been at the top of Holguin's list.'

Deborah cut in. 'It was obvious that a stolen vehicle was used for Lucy's abduction, then abandoned once she'd been delivered to a safe house. The bad news is that the security camera at your holiday complex, which should have picked up the vehicle either being driven onto the pitch-and-putt course or away from it, wasn't functioning that night. So no plates to go on. Wendy says the holiday complex's passive data collection systems are rubbish.'

Dave Williams took over. 'Malaga is saying that of the five missing Mazdas, three have now been recovered and another was a burnt-out wreck. None had any worthwhile evidence to link them with your little girl's abduction. So four down and one to go.'

'Where would they have taken our Lucy to, in this Mazda?'

'Probably somewhere in the city. It'll turn up abandoned either in the car park of a multiplex or a 24-hour supermarket with free parking. It's often several days before managers bother to report cars that haven't been moved. My guess is it's sitting outside an Aldi or a Lidl. If they were planning to move her somewhere else, they'd have used something bigger.'

'Somewhere else?'

'Andy, I'm afraid you and Doreen have got to face up to the fact that Lucy may no longer be in Spain.' But before he had time to fully digest this disturbing remark, Deborah checked her phone as it pinged. 'Ay up. My lord and master calls. I'd better be off folks. Catch up with you later, Andy.'

The men both wished her lucked as she marched smartly off with a blue plastic folder marked WAITROSE VISIT under her arm.

Andy returned to the theme of the missing Mazda. 'So let me get this straight: if there were only five hatchbacks missing that night; and if HOLMES is correct...'

Dave placed his hand lightly on Andy's wrist. 'Let me assure you, my friend, HOLMES is never wrong!'

'Sorry. So when this fifth Mazda does eventually turn up, its DNA evidence could be crucial.'

'Yes, DNA, clothes fibres, mud from the golf course on the floor mats. Even fingerprints; though I can't imagine they weren't wearing gloves the whole time.'

'They?'

'There were almost certainly two of them. The tyre marks tell us that. So if the Spanish police do decide to detain the Moroccan gardener, it will be a big step forward.'

But Dave Williams' hopes were short-lived. Standing beside the table was a short blonde girl in her early twenties, looking like a young Barbara Windsor.

'Hi Wendy. Meet Mr Wilmot. Andy this is our secretary Wendy Owen.' The girl gave Andy a warm smile before addressing the policeman.

'Bad news from Malaga, Dave.'

'What is it?'

'They released him on bail.'

'You're joking?'

'Wish I was. Holguin never responded to Deb's email this morning. So I've just rung my contact. She said the Guardia Civil went and picked him up at the resort at 8.30 a.m. and had him in for questioning for two hours.'

'Was the interview taped?'

'She didn't say. But she did say he'd accounted for his movements on the night of the abduction. They've confiscated his passport but released him.'

Dave Williams looked glumly at Andy Wilmot. 'Seems every time we take one step forward, the Spanish take two steps back. Deborah is NOT going to be best pleased, I can tell you.'

'Well there won't be any point in her reading Holguin the riot act when we tell her.'

'Why's that Wendy?'

'Because he's competing in a coppers-only golf tournament this afternoon'.

A few moments later a cheery Deborah returned. 'Well I must say that was short and sweet. I'm not sure he took much of it in. Kept going on about Palace protocol. That bloke's obsessed with getting his OBE before he steps down.'

Two burly motorcycle policemen took their seats at the next table and prepared to tuck into platefuls of bangers and mash. Deborah nodded to the older man. 'So…ready for next Saturday's big Camilla-fest, Barry?

'Don't talk to me about it, Debs. I've just had to cancel our annual family holiday in Cornwall.'

Sipping her coffee, the policewoman looked up at her silent assistant. 'Right Wend, got any glad tidings from Malaga for me? Don't tell me, they beat him unconscious then revived him so's he could sign a full confession?' She checked the three unsmiling faces around the table. She looked across at Dave Williams, raising her eyebrows. 'Bad news?'

'They released him.'

'They WHAT?'

Wendy spoke first. 'My Malaga contact tells me that the Moroccan gardener accounted for his movements last Friday night – claims he was in a tapas bar down at the harbour with his partner all evening. They've bailed him but confiscated his passport.'

Deborah banged her fist on the table, causing all the coffee beakers to jump. 'Fucking brilliant! He'll be halfway across Europe by now.' She slumped in her chair, staring at the spilt coffee. 'Wendy: pop upstairs and email your Malaga contact that I need to see a transcript of the gardener's interview asap, would you babes?' Wendy scampered off, glad to be away from the despondent trio.

Deborah gave her sergeant a wry smile. 'Rub of the green, old son?'

'Sorry Debs – football's my game, not crown bowls.'

'OK. Well our penalty shot just hit the cross-bar. Did you tell Andy here about the Press call our Media Unit got this morning?'

'Sorry, I hadn't got round to it. We were still on Holmes.'

'Fetch us another coffee, would you? Strong black.'

While the policeman was relieved to go and fetch a coffee for his boss, Deborah briefed Andy on an enquiry which had come in that morning from a local journalist. 'He's with a news agency which feeds the tabloids with Bedfordshire stories. This morning our Media Unit received a decidedly iffy call about the operation.'

'Maybe someone was on a fishing expedition.'

'Somehow I doubt it. One of the questions was: "Can you comment on the fact that a witness from Norfolk has come forward with some important new evidence?"'

'Blimey. And you only went up to Thetford two days ago. You don't suppose Wareing tipped them off?'

'He's not the type. Trust me.'

'Then how?'

'I'm afraid that phone hacking is still rife, Andy, despite all the vehement Press denials. We're just going to have to be extra careful when talking on mobile phones from now on. Right now, the last thing we want is to have all this splashed across the red tops.' The sergeant returned and placed a fresh polystyrene mug of black coffee in front of her. 'Thanks Dave. I know we're no closer to actually locating your daughter, which must be hugely frustrating for you and Doreen. But I know she's still alive. Every day that goes by without a ransom demand tells me that she's alive. I know it must seem bizarre to you as her distraught father, but no news is good news'. She looked across at her sergeant. 'Am I right, Dave?'

Scraping the last vestiges of treacle from the pudding bowl, Dave Williams nodded.

'While we're on the subject of phone calls – and this will apply to Doreen as well, especially if she's home alone. Mean-spirited scumbags - who can probably get your phone number from Directory Enquiries – may ring you and make nasty anonymous accusations.'

'What sort of accusations?'

'That you're both implicated in Lucy's disappearance. You'll probably start getting hate mail too.'

'You're joking!'

'Wish I was. Happens all the time, eh Dave?'

The sergeant nodded. ''fraid so. If I was you I'd book a call-minder service to screen all-incoming calls even before you answer.'

'Thanks, I'll get onto that later today. And I'll make sure to always open the post myself before Doreen is up.'

Deborah sipped her coffee. 'Andy, mind if I give it to you straight?'

'Sure.'

'From my perspective, I think you're holding up amazingly well. You're getting on with things and even these poxy setbacks haven't fazed you. But you're keeping Doreen in a sort of insulated cocoon. As a result, she seems to have given up all hope. It's as if she's thrown in the towel, emotionally. Believe me, that is one hundred per cent the wrong tack.'

'But how can you be so sure. Sure that we'll find Lucy?'

'Because this was a faultlessly-planned abduction. Not a spur of the minute child kidnapping by some twisted Spanish paedo. We've had no ransom demand; no items of Lucy's clothing have ever turned up; and there hasn't been a single reliable sighting. And I certainly don't count the tip-off that Gwent Police received last week. Some nutter only came into the station claiming he'd seen your daughter selling *The Big Issue* outside WH Smith in Newport!'

'Did you check it out?'

'Of course. The girl showed a constable her *Big Issue* sellers' ID. It was all kosher.'

'So what happened?'

'The station sergeant told the fellow that the maximum penalty for wasting police time was six months! I know it may sound weird to you as a law-abiding citizen, but to us coppers these are positive indicators, Andy.' Dave Williams nodded at her sagacity.

'You mustn't give up hope. Look at Kamiyah Mobley, stolen from a South Carolina maternity ward eight hours after she was born. Turned up seventeen years later. Or Zephany Nurse, the South African girl who was reunited with her parents after being kidnapped from hospital when she was two days old. Mrs Mobley and Mrs Nurse never gave up hope. That's what your Doreen should be doing. Not moping around, dosed up to the eyeballs on bloody Prozac.'

Andy was shocked by the young policewoman's forthright tone, but knew she was right. He glanced up at one of the canteen clocks. 'I guess I'd better be making tracks . Thanks for the lunch – and the pep talk'. He nodded across to Dave Williams, who stood up and shook him firmly by the hand. 'Good to meet you, Andy. Oh and by the way, I thought you'd like to know: all our screensavers upstairs have got that picture Geoff Evans took of your Lucy standing smiling, arm in arm with Jack Sparrow. You don't know how uplifting it makes us feel when we boot up every morning. It was Deborah's idea.' Andy smiled at this news.

'I'll see you out,' said Deborah standing up. They walked through reception and out into the visitors' car park. He unlocked the driver's door of the Mini Cooper and climbed in. To Andy's surprise, Deborah slipped into the passenger seat.

'Did you want a lift somewhere?'

'No, it's just I wanted to apologise, Andy, for speaking my mind a bit too freely in the canteen. Me and my big mouth again.'

'That's OK. And you're right about my cocooning Doreen. The fact is, Deborah, I've been between a rock and a hard place ever since we stepped on board that plane in Malaga. Doreen just couldn't wait to get away; to put as many miles between La Coveta and Milton Keynes as possible. Whereas I desperately wanted to stay, to be as close as possible to the investigation. The scene of that… despicable crime….' He lowered his head mid-sentence and sighed.

Deborah gazed through the windscreen and slowly shook her head. 'I know if I was running things down there in Malaga I'd be doing things differently.'

'In what way?'

'We get a prime tip-off from Norfolk and Holguin lets the suspect walk out of the station. Geoff Evans has provided us with a mug shot of the guy, but I bet it hasn't been circulated to Interpol yet. Why has it taken them nearly a fortnight to find a bloody hatchback? And your camera shots of Black Jacket, particularly the one of him watching you in the arrivals hall.'

'What about it?'

'That airport's got to be bristling with CCTV cameras – and unlike La Coveta's, I bet they're all working. So if Black Jacket arrived by car - probably a hire car – there could be images of him in one of the car parks, possibly even showing the car's plates. I'd have had a man checking the recording discs of all those car park cameras around the time of your flight's arrival. What d'you think Spain said when Dave emailed that idea to them?'

'Tell me.'

'"We'll look into it". Haven't heard a dicky bird. Like I said before, they're still deeply resentful towards us down there. When it comes to grudges, the Spanish have long memories - that's a Wendyism by the way.'

Deborah opened the car door and swung her legs out. 'Listen, I'd better let you go. Catch up with you later.'

Midway between Kempston and home, Andy heard his mobile phone ring in his pocket. He knew of a small country park along the route and pulled into its empty car park. He checked the 'missed call' message: it was Geoff Evans' number.

'Sorry I missed your call just now, Geoff; I was driving.'

'Hi mate. That's OK. All right to talk now?'

'Sure. I'm parked up.'

'So how's it all going? The investigation: Diane and I have been worried sick about you and Doreen, with all this garbage in the tabloids ever day. It's even got through to Anna, with kids at her school asking her about it.'

Andy took several deep breaths before answering. 'We're chasing our tails, mate. In a nutshell, we're no further forward. Deborah Tanner keeps telling me that no news is good news. Wish I could see it that way. And we're getting fuck-all support from the Spanish – though that British consular guy you found us in Malaga came up trumps getting us home.'

'Would you like me to come down for a few days? Maybe we could have a round of golf.'

'That's very kind of you, Geoff, but I'll OK. Anyway, school starts next week. First time I've ever been glad the summer holiday break was almost over! But Doreen really isn't coping at all well. Could you get Di to give her a call?

'Of course. Leave it to me, pal.'

'And thanks for sending over those pictures of the gardener.' He glanced through the windscreen at the tranquil landscape: a curved tree line surrounding a well-planted pool. A young woman emerged from a copse of silver birches, clasping the hand of an auburn-haired girl who looked about six yeas old. They walked, hand-in-hand, to the water's edge to feed some hungry ducks who were noisily heading towards them. Three weeks before, it could have been Doreen and Lucy.

'Still there, mate?'

Andy gulped hard, now fighting back the tears. 'Yup, sorry, Geoff. Just got a bit distracted. I'm fine at this end. If I need you to come down, I'll give you a shout.'

'Promise?'

'Promise.' He pressed the red button and began quietly sobbing.

~ ~ ~ ~ ~

Andy Wilmot got in just as the BBC Six O'clock TV news was beginning, with its brief coverage of Malaga developments omitting the arrest of the Moroccan gardener.

He stood in the hall but could detect no movement from their bedroom. He left a mug of tea by his sleeping wife's bedside and decided to make do with a cheese sandwich and an early night.

His phone pinged the arrival of an incoming message as he was washing up. *The fifth Mazda turned up this afternoon! Ring me in the morning. D*

Andy had a restless night with Mazda-crowded nightmares. He got up at 6.00am but managed to contain himself from ringing Deborah until 8.30pm, knowing that she would be at work at that hour.

'So tell me all about it. Where and when?'

'According to Wendy's friend in Holguin's office – I gather they get on so well because Wendy has fluent Spanish – it was collected from a Lidl car park at about 2 o'clock yesterday afternoon following a call from the manager of the supermarket. They've towed it to the city's forensics centre and were supposed to be examining it overnight. That's all I know, Andy. But it's a start.'

'I should say. Old Dave was on the money, wasn't he?'

'Bloody clairvoyant that one. So what have you got planned for today?'

'Well I've set up the call-minder service like you advised. And Doreen's got a doctor's appointment this afternoon, which her sister's going to take her to. I expect I'll do my school work here in the kitchen.'

'As soon as I hear anything from Malaga I'll call you.'

~ ~ ~ ~ ~

During a mid-morning coffee break, Andy wandered into the lounge at the rear of the bungalow – a room which he had barely set foot in since he and Doreen had returned from Spain.

They had inherited the bungalow from Doreen's parents, Jack and Doris Kennard, who had lived there after Jack retired from his job as a foreman joiner with the Cunard shipping line. Though the young couple had attempted to inject a more modern feel to the interior décor, the old lounge somehow got overlooked and was seldom used. The net curtains were from the 1950s, the faded purple three-piece suite still had its crocheted antimacasars and a dark-stained upright piano stood by the side of the cream-tiled fireplace. It was ordered and tidy, but felt unlived in.

Jack Kennard had died only one year before his wife; a year she spent mostly in the lounge, grieving his loss. Over the mantelpiece was a long oak-framed picture. It was a group photo showing at least thirty men, all in cloth caps and many wearing long aprons, lined up in two rows on a sloping bank. Behind them was the distinctive profile of the Queen Mary liner and standing proudly in the middle was pipe-smoking Jack Kennard.

Through the curtains of the bay window, Andy could see their young Indian neighbour Shanaya in the next door garden, watching her daughter practice with a skipping rope. Their little terrier barked excitedly.

He noticed that the extensive family photo collection on the long sideboard opposite the window had been rearranged. Several of his favourite pictures – all featuring Lucy in various phases of growing up – were missing. There wasn't a single close-up or group photograph with his daughter in it. Why on earth had Doreen removed them? He opened the long drawer of the sideboard and removed the leather-bound family photo album. The missing pictures were gathered together at the front in an envelope with old photos of Doreen's parents.

Distracted by the far-off ping of his iPhone, the puzzled father dashed back to the kitchen. MISSED CALL. He tapped in Deborah's number.

'Sorry I just missed your call. I was in another room.'

'No worries.'

'Well?'

'I'm still checking it through. It's a hurried Wendy translation of an email from Holguin which only arrived half an hour ago.'

'And?'

'They checked the car thoroughly and say they are certain that it was the one used in Lucy's abduction. The mud on the brake and clutch pedals exactly matches the soil samples from the hotel's pitch-and-putt course. It also says that on the floor of the boot there were minor traces of the same grade of chloroform which they'd detected on Lucy's pillow in your apartment.'

'So fairly conclusive.'

'Yes and no. They're claiming they found no fingerprints on the steering wheel, gear lever or door handles and no clothing fabric particles on the front seats. Frankly, I find that hard to believe. The mud and the sedative place the vehicle firmly at La Coveta. But we've still got no evidence as to who the driver or the accomplice were.'

'Would they have finger-printed the gardener when they had him in for questioning?'

'For sure. Or else they're even more incompetent than I thought.'

'DNA saliva swab?'

'I very much doubt it. He was barely at the station for two hours. It certainly wasn't recorded on the transcript of the interview.'

'So what's the next move, Deborah?'

'I'm not sure. I'm going to have a chat with Dave at lunchtime (he's out at the moment). There's isn't much he doesn't know about car crime. I'll call you this afternoon if that's OK?'

'Fine. I'll be here.'

Doreen Wilmot didn't appear until nearly 2 p.m. She looked bleary-eyed and was wearing no make-up. Andy made some fresh tea, while she sat silently at the kitchen table. 'What time is your sister calling to collect you?' he asked.

'At 2.45. My surgery appointment is for 3 p.m.'

He poured himself some tea and took a seat beside her. He was tempted to ask her about the mysterious disappearance of all Lucy's photographs, but refrained. 'What are you going to tell the doctor?'

She stared into her half-empty mug of tea and sighed. 'I'm going to have to tell him I can't go back to work yet. And ask if he'll change my medication. The pills he gave me are just making things worse.'

'Talk to Sheila in the surgery waiting room, why don't you? She's been in nursing all her life.' Doreen Wilmot nodded and went to the hall to get her coat.

A car pulled up outside just as it was getting dark, but Sheila didn't accompany her sister into the bungalow. Andy met his wife in the hallway.

'Come inside and tell me how you got on'.

Without removing her coat, Doreen Wilmot wandered into the kitchen and slumped down in her usual chair. 'Not much to tell, really. He renewed my prescription and said he's going to refer me to see a psychotherapist at the hospital. But as they're snowed under with appointments, I could be waiting up to four weeks.'

'So not much help there.' She shook her head disconsolately.

'And what did Sheila say when you were waiting at the surgery to go in to see the doctor?'

'Not a lot really.'

Her husband moved round to stand behind his wife and placed a hand gently on her shoulder. She slouched forwards. 'Perhaps we could get Diane Evans to come down? Geoff says she'd be happy to stay as I've got school starting next week.' The suggestion was greeted with a slow shake of the head.

Andy sensed that Doreen was pretty close to breaking down in floods of tears again. He moved to the cooker to make her a drink. 'Shall I make you a hot water bottle?' She shook her head, which was now half-way to touching the table top.

'Please don't take this the wrong way, Doreen, but when I was at the police headquarters today, the staff there all urged me – us, that is – to take a positive view on what's happened since Lucy went missing. Not to give up hope....' Cutting him short, Doreen Wilmot snapped: 'By "staff", I take it you mean your silver-haired fancy woman!' She stomped from the room.

V

Spoils of War

AAMIR KASHANI had made himself a hurried breakfast of toast and instant coffee, ahead of the arrival of his garrulous Cuban housekeeper Audrey, who was always at her most talkative first thing in the morning. His phone signalled an incoming text from Roland, his driver. *Am parked outside now.*

It was two minutes before 8a.m. when the carpet dealer summoned the lift. It arrived empty and, much to his relief, didn't stop at any intermediate floors before arriving in the entrance hall. Lift conversations at the best of times were tiresome; at eight in the morning they were insufferable. He often recalled with dread a one-sided exchange he had had with the tower's long-time resident Arthur Scargill, an experience which cemented his hatred of the trade union movement.

Behind his desk Malcolm X was slouched forward asleep, his shaved head resting on the desk top. Kashani made a mental note to send a letter of complaint to the management committee. It was bitingly cold when he stepped out onto the cobbled forecourt. Roland stood to attention beside the black Lexus. He wore a high-buttoned vintage-style chauffeur's coat, over black twill trousers. His dark blue peaked hat bore a large gold 'K' on the cap badge. Saluting, he swung the rear door of the limousine open. 'Shoreditch, Mr Kashani?'

'Yes please, Roland. You can leave me there, as I shall probably take most of the morning checking the new consignment.'

'Very good, Sir.' They moved away from the tower and into the long road tunnel which runs up to Moorgate underground station. City commuters were already streaming out. The chauffeur comfortably navigated the journey northwards to the borders of Islington within a quarter of an hour.

The only distinguishing sign above the security key pad which activated the entrance door to the building were the letters 'K C'. Kashani Carpets did not intend to advertise its presence in this twilight area of London. He let the door swing shut and automatically lock itself then descended the concrete steps. The light behind the glass panel of the store's entrance door indicated that his assistant Tomas Pavlovic was already at work.

The basement was a low-ceilinged, pristine-clean space, more like a laboratory than an oriental carpet warehouse. It was lit from above by a grid of pavement lights, supplemented by two narrow bands of shaded neon tubes hanging above parallel workbenches with white laminate tops.

The precise organisation and regimented layout of the basement workspace reflected the owner's borderline OCD condition. Neat stacks of labelled rugs were set against an unplastered wall and the heady odour of the rugs' plant-based dyes suffused the atmosphere like a souk. Aamir Kashani's desk was set in one of the two brick-lined vaults of the old cellar. The adjoining vault was completely filled by a huge safe. On the far corner of the desk, in shadow, was a framed photo of his daughter Alice, sitting in front of a smiling Marta Kashani, on the galloper of a fairground carousel.

Mounted at an angle on the back wall of this vault and lit by a solitary spotlight, was a Perspex box, measuring about one metre square. Inside was a small model made of card and wire. It depicted a flat-roofed, single-storey L-shaped building, set beside a matching L-shaped swimming pool. The base of the box was labelled: "VILLA EANNA, KYRENIA. Client: A.Kashani".

He addressed a stocky youth who was kneeling on the floor. 'Good morning, Tomas. Making an early start?'

'Morning Mr Kashani. Yes, I thought I'd get on with sorting yesterday's consignment.'

'Good idea. Did it all go smoothly?'

'Fine. Stansted's a whole lot easier than Heathrow, though the extra mileage is a nuisance. I didn't get back here until 11 p.m.'

'Less checks?'

'Far fewer. We sailed through. The staff are far more obliging than those Wallies out at Heathrow. And far fewer armed police up in Essex, though they did put a sniffer dog into the back of the van at the last checkpoint.'

Kashani carefully considered the remark. The thought of having his newly-imported carpets checked was not a concern; but he wondered whether highly-trained police dogs might be curious about rare Mesopotamian artefacts. He resolved to request that in all future shipments they should be triple-wrapped.

Tomas continued to remove the coiled carpets and rugs from their cylindrical cardboard tubes, carefully unrolling them on the floor to reveal rows of small bubble-wrapped antiques concealed in the core. 'I've left a message on your desk, Mr Kashani. A Mr Murphy telephoned last night just as I was leaving. He asked if you'd call him this morning.'

'Thank you, Tomas.' Kashani moved across to his private alcove. A telephone number was written on a Post-it fixed to the corner of his leather-bound blotter. Despite Tomas's scrupulous discretion, he would have preferred to have made the call in private, but was anxious to hear Ted Murphy's news.

He picked up the desk phone and tapped in the number. The ringing tone indicated a foreign location.

'Ted? Aamir. I believe you rang last night.'

'Top of the morning to you,' came a cheerful Irish salutation down the line.

'So, do you have some good news for me?'

'Good and bad. Which do you want first?'

Without hesitating, the carpet dealer replied: 'Let's get the bad news out of the way first.'

'Right you be. Well one branch of the family — the children, actually — don't want to sell.'

'But that's crazy! The building plot is for sale. It says so in as many words in Turkish on the board there.'

'I know, I know. It's the daughter who's putting up the objection.'

'On what grounds?'

'You're not Turkish. She's saying that she'll only give her formal consent to a sale to a Turk. What's more, an islander and not someone from the mainland.'

'But that's ridiculous. Narrow-minded and perverse.'

'I agree entirely, my friend.'

'Could she be…induced to change her mind, do you think?'

'If you mean what I think you mean, I'd say no. In her book, national pride comes before Euros.'

'I see. Let me reflect on it will you, Ted?'

'Certainly. Do you want the good news?'

'Of course.'

'The Mayor is "on board"'.

Kashani gave a half-smile and glanced across to note that Tomas was now out of earshot. He looked up at the model of his new villa. 'All departments?'

'Yup. Planning, building regulations and highways.'

'Highways? I don't intend building a motorway up to my villa, you know.'

'According to the Mayor, the present track isn't wide enough.'

'Wide enough for what?'

'Ambulances and fire engines, would you believe?'

'Allah protect me from bureaucratic regulation! So the Brussels mania for red tape has spread as far as the eastern Mediterranean, has it?'

'Seems so. Don't forget Turkey would like to join the club one day. You'll just have to go along with him. Keep him sweet.'

'I thought I'd 'sweetened' him enough already. That Kazak runner I gave him is worth over six grand.'

'Though I don't suppose you paid a tenth of that for it.'

'That's beside the point. I'm a dealer, Ted. That's what dealers do.'

'So am I to tell him "yes" to all three?'

'I suppose so,' replied Kashani grudgingly. 'Will it cost?'

'Just the local council's usual scale of charges. Plus 10 per cent of course.'

'And I don't need to ask where that 10 per cent will be going.'

'So it's just little Miss Awkward we've got to worry about now. Get back to me when you've thought of a way round that problem, will you Aamir? And don't leave it too long.'

Kashani (who resolutely refused to take orders from others) snapped back: 'Why the hurry?'

'The hurry my friend is because Kyrenia is experiencing what can only be described as a Russian invasion. You wouldn't recognise the old harbour from when you were last here.'

'Really?'

'Really. It isn't a quaint little Cypriot fishing port any longer, you know – it's being turned into a fucking marina for multi-million-dollar ocean-going yachts! Last week we even had Deripaska's floating palace calling in. Probably to check the berthing charges.'

Kashani hung up without replying – a discourteous trait he often employed in his telephone conversations when offended. He got up and walked across to inspect Tomas's labours. Eight small plastic parcels were set in a neat row on the floor against the newly-arrived stack of carpets and rugs, each of which had been folded and labelled.

'Are the parcels to go into the safe unopened, Mr Kashani?'

'Yes please, Tomas. I'll try to take a look at them over the weekend. I like to come down here on a Saturday afternoon when I won't be disturbed.'

'Of course, Sir.'

The true reason for Kashani's secretiveness was that though his assistant was aware that items were being smuggled into the country inside the carpets, he had no idea of their provenance or value.

The dealer checked his watch. 'Perhaps you'd like to go upstairs for your mid-morning coffee now.' It wasn't so much a suggestion as a formal instruction. The youth duly slipped on his leather jacket and left. At last Aamir Kashani was alone with his latest treasure trove.

Via a carefully coded email, he had been advised that the eight pieces included in the new Stansted consignment were some of the most valuable of all the items which he had ever imported. He picked up the smallest item and gingerly peeled off its outer layer of bubble-wrap. The gleam of dull bronze could be seen through the plastic. The cylindrical item was going to be about five inches high and half that in diameter. It was very heavy - solid bronze he surmised. The top had a pointed end.

Like a child at Christmas, he slowly removed the last of the covering.

Aamir Kashani stared in wonder at the object which nestled in his left hand. It was a bronze male figure, clad in a full-length pleated robe, probably a priest he suspected, as his long beard was neatly 'crimped' in parallel horizontal curls. The man's left hand – bent at the elbow – held some sort of globe, while his right hand grasped a long slender rod, which reached above his head. But it was the

verdigris patina on the pleats of the priest's robe which was so
striking. Matt, unblemished and at least 3500 years old.

Hearing the street door slam shut, the carpet dealer hastily
wrapped the figure up in its plastic protection and sealed it with
some adhesive tape from the dispenser on his desk. He managed
to place the small item back in the row on the floor as Tomas re-
entered. Kashani was still stunned by the beauty of the object he
had just been handling.

By mid-afternoon the Pakistani entrepreneur (and would-be
property developer) believed he had resolved the Kyrenia building
site problem. He rang Ted Murphy back.

'I say, Aamir, you don't let the grass grow under your feet, do
you?'

'You implied urgency, this morning.'

'So what's it to be?'

'Ask the daughter who's objecting if she will consider selling the
site to a Turkish nominee of my choosing. An islander. The transaction
can be handled by an *Avukat* in Nicosia, with the purchaser meeting
the legal costs of both sides.'

'I think I can see where you're coming from, you crafty old devil.
Twelve months after the sale has gone through, you'll re-purchase
the land from your nominee.'

'Precisely'. Kashani turned to look lovingly at the small model of
his Cyprus villa. The transaction was back on.

Two hours later, just as he was preparing to leave his warehouse,
the Irishman called back.

'I'm afraid we've missed the boat, old son.'

'How do you mean?'

'When I telephoned Miss Awkward this morning straight after
our conversation, she informed me that yesterday the family agreed
a sale to a Mr Aksanov.'

Kashani pursed his lips. After a long pause he murmured 'I see. And is he a local like she wanted?'

'He's no more Turkish than I am. He's an oligarch (big in gas pipeline production) whose Russian name happens to have Turkish origins.'

Kashani replaced the handset without replying. He switched off the light over the model of his dreamed-of Cyprus villa that was not to be and trudged up the stairs to await Roland's arrival.

THE CONVENT OF THE SACRED ORDER OF THE BLESSED SISTERS
OF THE IMMACULATE CONCEPTION

VI

Lucerne

LUCY AWOKE in a white room. Purest white. Bathed in sunshine. The walls were white, the ceiling was white and the bed sheets and cover were white. Even the light shade, high up in the ceiling was white. Apart from the bed the only other item of furniture was a small pine table.

By raising her head slightly the girl could see a large rectangular sash window beyond the end of the bed. It framed a beautiful view of a lake, with snow-capped mountains in the distance.

Turning her head slightly to one side on her pillow, Lucy saw that a young nun was seated at her bedside. She too was clad entirely in white. Her eyes were closed and her head was bowed, as if in prayer. In her lap she clasped a small wooden crucifix. Sensing Lucy's movement, the nun opened her eyes and looked up. She had a sublime face, with a soft pink complexion and penetrating blue eyes. She smiled but didn't speak.

'Am I in Heaven?' Lucy asked.

The nun gave her a lovely warm smile. 'No, my child. You are only in the convent's Sanatorium. You were exhausted after your long journey.'

'Journey from where?'

'We weren't told.'

'And are my parents here? And where is my friend Anna?'

The nun bowed her head, contemplating her crucifix. 'You came alone.'

'Where did I come from?'

'We weren't told.'

Lucy set her head back onto the pillow and closed her eyes. Though any precise memory of what had happened to her before this moment was impossible to grasp clearly, she could vaguely recall a long bumpy journey in a big car, through which she had slept intermittently. She remembered being carried and laid into the vehicle as rain was falling. Of being bundled up and carried from the vehicle, as a bell tolled, into an echoing building, surrounded by silent people.

Lucy turned to look again at the praying nun. What is this place called?'

'You are in the Sanatorium of the Convent of the Sacred Order of the Blessed Sisters of the Immaculate Conception.' The nun was softly spoken, with her answers almost whispers.

'Is this a hospital?'

'A sanatorium is like a hospital. This is a convent and also a finishing school.'

'What's a finishing school?'

'It is a place where girls are trained to become ladies.'

'Where are we?'

'Lucerne.'

'Where's that?'

'In Switzerland, *meien liebchen*.'

Confused by all this information and long words, Lucy closed her eyes and drifted back to sleep.

~ ~ ~ ~ ~

The silence of Lucy's first days in the lakeside sanatorium were only disturbed by the arrival of light food, which came on an old-fashioned trolley pushed by another nun clad in white. Her seated guardian would receive these meals and place them on a tray covered by a white damask napkin. Breakfast was usually muesli and fruit segments, though occasionally a soft-boiled egg appeared. Lunch would be a nourishing salad, accompanied by bread and butter and at supper time she would be offered a hot pasta dish. Spaghetti was her favourite.

The evening meal trolley would arrive at sunset, often coinciding with the tolling of a bell. Supper's soporific effect invariably induced eight or ten hours of sleep. The nun in white was always at her bedside when she awoke in the morning.

On the third day Lucy asked when she would be allowed to get up. 'Perhaps tomorrow *meine liebchen.*' The nun was carefully combing Lucy's dark hair. 'You were very exhausted when you arrived and Mother Superior instructed that you should have complete rest and not be disturbed.'

'Mother Superior?'

'The Abbess of this convent, whom we all serve.'

'And what is your name?'

'I am Sister Beatrice. I am only a Novice.' Beatrice glanced down at the crucifix which lay in her lap.

'What's a Novice?'

'A Novice is a young woman who aspires to one day become a nun.'

Having finished her breakfast, Lucy was keen to learn more about convents and nuns and novices and abbesses. But Sister Beatrice – having returned the tray to the trolley – quietly resumed her seat by the bed and lowered her head in prayer. The provision of information to the little girl was being carefully rationed, it seemed.

Lucy slipped into a half-sleep, illuminated by images of a watery cave. She stirred as she felt the young nun's finger being run gently along the bridge of her nose. The girl opened her eyes.

'Your freckles are so sweet, little one.'

'I hate them!'

'Why is that?'

'Because they're not like my friend Anna's. Hers are in two little clusters on each side of her nose, while mine are scattered all over the place!'

The novice smiled. "And do you know the legend of how freckles first came about?'

'No. Do tell me.'

Beatrice gave a little giggle. 'Well, of course, it is a pagan story and I am sure Mother Vanessa would be very cross if she knew I had told it to you...'

'Go on!' urged Lucy, now sitting up attentively in bed.

'Well...the Irish people once lived far away, down in Greece. They were called Gaels – which is where the name of their Gaelic language comes from. It seems they were getting homesick and one of the Gods said to their leader: "We shall scatter stardust onto your faces - on either side of your noses – like a miniature celestial map, showing where your homeland is. So you will never be homesick again." Lucy smiled, closed her eyes and soon fell asleep, puzzling over what 'celestial' meant.

~ ~ ~ ~ ~

Lucy soon realised that the routine of the convent was governed by the sound of bells. Not always the same bell. Several bells, in various locations with different tones, seemed to ring out the orders of the day.

The view from her bedroom window of the vast lake, the snow-capped mountains and the dazzling azure skies remained virtually unchanged from day to day, though very occasionally – distantly – she would pick up the sound of children's voices. Sometimes these sounds came from outside – as if children were playing, out of her sight, somewhere down in the convent's gardens. Sometimes a more echoing sound suggested that the youngsters were inside the building, perhaps marching along a long corridor.

After her breakfast on the fourth morning of her confinement, Lucy learned that Sister Beatrice had to attend Mass. The news was accompanied by the pealing of several bells. 'I have brought you an English book to read,' the young nun told her. 'It's the story of a bear named Rupert. I shall return in time to bring you your lunch. On Sundays we always have a hot meal.'

The melodic peal of bells was replaced by the sound of a more sombre solitary bell. Lucy guessed that Sunday Mass was probably about to begin. She cautiously slid back the bedclothes and walked over to the window to try to discover more of her new home.

Her room in the sanatorium was very high up. Several floors below, she could make out a long expanse of neatly-mown grass, divided by a shingle path. In the distance, the path arrived at the huge entrance doors of what looked like a church. Above its doors was a circular stained glass window.

Immediately to the right of the convent church the lawns ran right down to the edge of the lake. There was no beach or pathway, nor any sign of people walking by the water's edge. The sole foreground feature – stark and slightly frightening – was a huge blackened timber cross, like a giant version of the crucifix which Sister Beatrice wore around her neck. The big cross cast a long shadow across the lawns. Russet tints on the leaves of a group of trees indicated the approach of autumn.

But it was the church building's slender circular spire which fascinated Lucy. Tapering as it rose up, its sides were decorated in zig-zag pattern of dark grey metal with its top surmounted by an ornate weather-vane. At a distance, it was hard to make out what the statue represented, though she could see that it was an angel with golden wings. Looming above the spire was a pair of gaunt brick bell towers. Lucy resolved to ask Sister Beatrice for an explanation later. She returned to her bed to enjoy the adventures of Rupert the Bear.

Lucy heard the familiar rattling sound of her meal trolley approaching her bedroom door and the sound of two women talking. The door opened to reveal Sister Beatrice accompanied by another smiling novice who was introduced as Sister Serina. The stranger was of about the same age as her companion, with wisps of dark hair peeping from beneath her headdress.

Sister Beatrice set three places for lunch on the table at the window, while the newcomer sat on the edge of the bed. 'I'm very pleased to meet you, Lucy. Sister Beatrice has told me all about you and about the excellent progress you've made since your arrival last week.' Lucy could make out the aroma of a casserole and began to feel terribly hungry.

After a trifle and custard dessert, Lucy broached the subject of getting up. The two novices looked at each other, before Beatrice replied: 'I intend to speak to Mother Vanessa this evening before *Compline*, Lucy. Perhaps I may have some good news for you when I bring you your breakfast tomorrow.'

Pleased with this response, and given the friendly atmosphere, the English girl decided to find out a little more about her surroundings. Glancing out of the window she asked Sister Serina: 'What is that big wooden cross down by the lake?'

'That's our Calvary Cross, Lucy. It represents the cross on which Our Lord was crucified.' She glanced towards her fellow novice. 'It's a much larger version of the crucifix which Sister Beatrice always wears.' She hooked up a small gold cross on a chain which she was wearing. 'Did you know hers came from Gaza?' Beatrice was clutching it in one hand.

'Where's Gaza?'

'In Palestine. I was teaching in a school there. The pupils made this for me out of olive wood as a farewell gift.'

Lucy glanced back out of the window in the direction of the convent chapel, whose doors were now swung open, with several nuns standing in the entrance porch talking. The nun in the centre of the group had a black headdress and a distinctive black silk shawl over her shoulders.

'What is the meaning of the statue right at the top of the church spire?' Lucy asked.

The two novices exchanged knowing smiles. Sister Beatrice then volunteered a succinct explanation of the lofty figure. 'Well Lucy, you have heard me speak of the name of this Order, haven't you?'

Lucy nodded.

'Can you remember what it is?'

Lucy recalled that it was a long and complicated set of words, some of which she didn't fully understand. 'This is the Convent of the Sisters...'

'Blessed Sisters...'

'The Convent of the Blessed Sisters...of the Sacred Order...'

'Very good *meine liebchen*!'

'...of the err...Conception. Except I don't know what conception means.'

'The Immaculate Conception' corrected Sister Serina. 'That is something that I expect Sister Irma will be telling you all about in your biology classes.'

Lucy pointed towards the spire. 'And who is that with the gold wings?'

'That is the Angel Gabriel,' Sister Beatrice added. 'He was God's messenger who came down from Heaven to tell Mary that she was to give birth to baby Jesus.'

Lucy was slightly baffled by the complexity of the nuns' Bible story and was starting to feel tired from her big lunch. Sensing this, Sister Serina led her by the hand back to bed, while Sister Beatrice stacked their lunch things onto the trolley. Then the two young women tucked her sheets up to her neck and slipped quietly out.

Lucy's last thought before falling asleep was that she would so like to have them both as older sisters.

~ ~ ~ ~ ~

For her breakfast the following morning Sister Beatrice brought Lucy a soft-boiled egg - and the news she had been so wanting to hear. 'Mother Vanessa says you may get up after you have had your breakfast. She has asked me to take you downstairs, where she would like to talk to you.'

'What about?'

'I must leave that for the Mother Superior. But I imagine she will be explaining to you things like your classes, your dormitory and of course the services in our chapel.'

'Classes?'

'But of course, my child. We have both your education and your spiritual wellbeing to consider.'

'And will there be other children in my dormitory?'

'*Natürlich*.'

Under the breakfast trolley was a change of clothes for Lucy. She slipped into a white T-shirt, blue denim jeans and a pair of pale blue trainers.

The corridor outside her bedroom was cold, lofty and only dimly lit by tall narrow windows. Each contained a small circular stained glass image of a religious figure – many with golden haloes. At the end of the corridor was a long winding staircase, its irregular steps formed by well-worn bricks. A thick rope, hanging in loops from the wall, was the hand rail.

After descending two levels the pair arrived in a huge octagonal hallway, lit by a brass chandelier. The scent of stooks of drying lavender, set in copper urns, suffused the atmosphere, merging with the incense from the chapel.

They walked along another deserted and echoing passageway until they reached an arched doorway marked 'Calefactory'. They entered a lovely long warm space, lit by candles, where two parallel rows of cushioned seats were set below panelled walls. A well-worn hessian mat ran down the centre of the room. At the far end was a huge log fire, with piles of logs stacked neatly on either side. Above the fireplace hung an old oil painting of a Pope. There was no-one else in the room.

While they awaited the arrival of the Abbess, Lucy's guardian explained to her exactly what a Calefactory was. 'The words come from the Latin meaning "warming house"', she said.

'In olden times, convents like ours here – and monasteries too, for that matter - had no form of heating whatsoever. So, as you can imagine, they were extremely cold places to live in in winter. Especially in somewhere like Switzerland! The bedrooms – we call them cells – were unheated too. So nuns and monks were permitted to come to these special rooms to warm themselves between the services. But they weren't supposed to talk.'

'Why was that?'

'Most convents are known as "silent orders", meaning nuns must not talk to each other, but save all their words for prayer. Ours is a Carmelite Order.'

The novice's explanations were cut short by the arrival of the Abbess. She had a stout build and was wearing the distinctive silk shawl and headdress which Lucy had seen from her bedroom window after the Sunday Mass. The three sat together beside the fire, but their conversation was stilted and formal. While talk with Beatrice up in her bedroom had been relaxed and informal – almost sisterly – Mother Vanessa kept her new charge very much at arm's length. Beatrice remained silent throughout, holding her olive wood crucifix in her lap.

'You will be in a dormitory – overseen by Sister Beatrice here – with fourteen other girls. Sister will introduce them all to you tonight after supper. The two services which you will be expected to attend are *Prime* before breakfast and *Compline* after supper. All our meals, which we have together in the convent's Refectory, are taken in silence.'

The big woman stood, indicating that the interview was at an end. The unsmiling Abbess then handed Lucy a small folded blue card. 'Sister Beatrice will explain the academic subjects listed in here to you later.' With which the Abbess turned and departed.

Lucy glanced down at the card she was clutching. A gold-coloured image of the Angel Gabriel was set above six embossed letters: "BSSOIC". She gave Beatrice a bemused look. She was really no wiser as to where she had come from; why she was being kept here; or when – if ever – she would be leaving Switzerland.

The girl was to enjoy the peaceful luxury of her bedroom in the sanatorium for only one more night. Having given her a cursory run-through of the classes which were to begin the following morning, Sister Beatrice left after their shared supper. The young nun kissed her on the forehead. 'Sleep well, *meine liebchen*.'

But sleep didn't come easily this night. Half-awake and half-asleep, the little lost girl tried desperately to recall earlier times. Memories of her parents seemed to be fading fast, overtaken by the stern images imposed by the convent's tightly-ordered regime, the unsmiling nuns and its austere interiors. Sister Beatrice was her sole consolation. But even she was reluctant to tell Lucy where she had come from or who had brought her to this strange place.

~ ~ ~ ~ ~

The bell for *Prime* began ring at 5.45am. Lucy hurriedly washed and dressed and set off for the long winding staircase she had descended with Sister Beatrice the day before. In the big hallway a gaggle of boys and girls was lining up ready to process in pairs to the chapel service. Two nuns beckoned the crocodile to move forwards. Lucy took up the rear, alongside a dark-skinned boy in a wheelchair.

They entered the chapel and the children filed into two rows of pews facing the altar. Lucy counted 28 figures, with ages ranging (she guessed) from six to ten. With her neighbour in the wheelchair that meant there were 30 children altogether living here in the convent. Fifteen boys and fifteen girls. They knelt to pray, giving Lucy a chance to peep between her hands at the other boys and girls.

The service was entirely in Latin. No hymns were sung, though the assembled nuns, seated in facing choir stalls flanking the altar, recited two psalms. After a blessing by the Abbess they filed out – Lucy taking up the rear and pushing the wheelchair - and the column headed towards the convent's Refectory.

This was a lofty hall beneath an elaborately-constructed timber roof. Seated on a raised platform at the end were about a dozen nuns and novices (including Sisters Beatrice and Serina). This top table was overseen by the Abbess, seated in a tall throne-like chair, again decorated with an image of the Angel Gabriel. Two servants in white uniforms appeared from a side door, first serving the Abbess and nuns, and then leaving bowls of mixed muesli at the end of the two refectory tables where the children sat. A Latin grace was said by the Abbess and then the whole assembly began to eat breakfast in silence.

~ ~ ~ ~ ~

After breakfast, Lucy hurriedly snatched a few words with the boy in the wheelchair. His name was Nazri and he came from Libya. Like Lucy he was a recent arrival. Half of his right leg was missing. As she pushed him out into the long gloomy corridor, he told her that their first lesson that morning was to be Religious Studies. This would be followed by Art. 'And because there are so many nationalities here, all the lessons are in English.' Then it would be lunchtime. Brightening up, Nazri said: 'Then we get half-an-hour off before afternoon lessons. If it's fine we usually go in the gardens and play volleyball. Do you want to come?'

'Yes please!' Lucy had made a new friend.

~ ~ ~ ~ ~

At her first morning's class in Religious Education, Lucy learned that the Liturgy of the Hours was the Catholic Church's official set of nine services of prayer, spaced through the day. Only the nuns were obliged to rise for *Lauds* (at 3 a.m), though all pupils were expected to be washed and dressed to go down to *Prime* at 6 o'clock. The Catechism, they were sternly assured by the old nun instructing them, would be a central part of their religious education at Lucerne. Lucy rolled her eyes in a swivel making Nazri grin.

Art, with Miss Morrison was an altogether different matter. To start with, the teacher wasn't a nun, but an Englishwoman dressed in ordinary clothes, under a paint-splattered smock.

The young art teacher pinned a huge picture of brightly-coloured swirls and splashes onto the classroom blackboard. 'Now I don't expect you to remember the name of the artist who made this picture: he was an American named Jackson Pollock. He believed in the freedom of expression that we should have when we paint our pictures.'

Moving through the class, Miss Morrison set down six small paint tubes in front of each of her pupils.

'Please open the art books on your desks at a clean page and gently squeeze out some of the colours from the tubes, so that they make interesting shapes. Like the one on the blackboard. Take your time.'

Squeals of delight followed this invitation to enjoy free-style abstract art for the first time. Lucy's picture was adjudged by

Miss Morrison to be the best and was pinned up alongside Jackson Pollock's. Then the happy class filed out for lunch in the Refectory.

As Nazri had predicted, the half-hour post-lunch recreation session – no doubt fired up by Miss Morrison's abstract art session – was a joyful free-for-all. Lucy was starting to get settled in.

Following supper in the Refectory, Sister Beatrice led Lucy by the hand up the long staircase to their L-shaped attic dormitory. Sixteen narrow beds were set beneath the eaves, with four small dormer windows let into the sloping ceiling. Most of the dormitory's young inhabitants had already arrived and were sitting on the ends of their beds, wearing pyjamas or nightdresses. They greeted Sister Beatrice warmly as she entered. Lucy realised that her dormitory monitor was well-liked.

The novice stood in the doorway holding Lucy's hand. 'Good evening, children. I want you to meet Lucy, who arrived at our convent a few days ago. Please make her feel welcome, will you, as being all alone in a strange foreign place can be very hard to cope with at first.' The smiles and spontaneous clapping which greeted this announcement made Lucy feel touched and elated and at the end of a long and often perplexing day, the girl was glad to climb into the bed next to Sister Beatrice and fall asleep.

~ ~ ~ ~ ~

In terms of friendships and mutual support, the inhabitants of the two dormitories (Leo and Pius), located in opposite wings within the convent, tended to keep within their own spheres. So it was that Lucy soon found herself, in Pius, amongst an interesting cosmopolitan collection of 14 girls, from eight countries.

In the next bed to her on one side was Russian Saskia and next to her was little La Na from China, the daughter of a diplomat who worked in Washington. La Na had a passion for graphic novels of Agatha Christie mysteries. By torchlight one night Lucy and Saskia read one of La Na's comic books called *Murder on the Orient Express*, a thrilling murder mystery on a train, with loads of suspects and clues to solve. Saskia quickly decided who the murderer was; but cautious Lucy hadn't made up her mind. 'Suppose there's more than one murderer?' she asked her companion as they both went to sleep.

A spirited German girl named Anika (a natural-born leader who Lucy was soon to learn the nuns regarded as a trouble-maker) was in the bed opposite. It was Anika's firm belief that the Lucerne convent was a silent order not simply because the nuns never talked to each other, but because they were almost certainly hiding lots of secrets.

Next to Anika was a French orphan named Bernadette. As Lucy was later to discover, Bernadette was a bit of a swot who could always be relied upon to whisper the right answers in classroom exams. In the far corner of the dormitory – and always the most talkative after lights-out – were four noisy girls from Kuwait, who had been nicknamed the Brat Pack. The other six children in Pius were from Oman, Japan and Saudi Arabia. Though talking after lights-out was officially forbidden, easygoing Sister Beatrice usually allowed the children to whisper.

Lucy's one regret was that because of his wheelchair her new friend Nazri had to sleep alone in a ground floor room, though she often made up for his absence by going downstairs early so that she could push him to Refectory for breakfast.

Nazri didn't talk much about his disability save to say that it occurred at the start of the Libyan conflict when he and his parents were fleeing from the city of Tripoli, which was being bombarded by NATO air strikes. He was certain that it was thanks to the prompt action of medics from Médecins sans Frontières that his life was saved, following a bomb explosion in the street they were fleeing down. His parents, who survived the attack, had moved to Zurich to be near him and regularly visited their son at the convent. Much of the brave little Libyan boy's story was told to Lucy while they sat together in the gardens one sunny morning before classes began.

'And have your parents decided to remain in Zurich?' Lucy asked.

'Yes, there's no going back. Our house in Tripoli was reduced to rubble. And there's little chance of stability until Colonel Gaddafi has gone.'

'What does your Dad do?'

'He's an engineer. Now he's working in Zurich for VBZ. That's the company that runs the city's tram system.'

'Bonding' with her instructors at the Lucerne convent was less easy for Lucy. The nuns were especially formal in their classroom manner and uniformly strict with all pupils. One or two of the non-religious teachers - such as Miss Morrison - were always fun to be with. Like the two novices who had looked after Lucy since her arrival, nuns' habits were white and starched, with beige brown veils over their white coifs

The convent's three most senior nuns (all with teaching experience from the outside world or teaching degrees) were strict and serious at all times. These were: Sister Naomi (Ancient History and Religious Education), Sister Martha (Politics and World Economics) and Sister Irma (Science and Biology). Lucy soon noticed that this trio would always sit close by Mother Vanessa at Refectory meals - often whispering - suggesting that they were probably her chief advisors. It was Bernadette who shrewdly advised Lucy never to answer them back.

~ ~ ~ ~ ~

After breakfast one Saturday morning, Sister Beatrice was waiting outside the Refectory. Lucy and Saskia came out together intending to go for a walk in the convent grounds where Lucy was keen to study the Calvary Cross at close quarters. A cross without a Jesus troubled her. The young nun was carrying three pairs of scissors tied by a cord to her wrist.

She asked the girls if they would like to help her pick early-season redcurrants in the vegetable gardens. She told them that the convent's kitchens would be making them into jams to sell in Lucerne.

It was a gloriously sunny morning when Lucy and Saskia reached the vegetable garden. In the shadow of the chapel spire were two clearly defined growing areas, one for vegetables and the other for soft fruit. These were dissected by a narrow grass path, at the end of which was a small timber-clad potting shed. This was the private domain of old Joseph, the convent's gardener, though Saturday was Joseph's day off.

The novice led the way through an iron entrance gate and along the central pathway. Pointing out the redcurrant bushes which were glistening with dew, she presented both girls with an ancient wooden trug in which she had placed a pair of scissors.

'Unlike lifting potatoes or onions, cropping redcurrants is easy-peasy,' Beatrice enthused. 'You should soon have these trugs filled, girls; then you can go for your walk.' The three silently set to work with their scissors and within half an hour their wooden baskets were filled to overflowing with the crop. They stopped to take a short break.

'Lucy, be a dear and pop down to Joseph's shed and collect some cardboard punnets for us would you?' Beatrice asked. 'The shed isn't locked.'

Lucy ambled along the pathway towards the old green shed. Even at ten o'clock in the morning there was still dew on the grass path. She eased back the iron bolt of the shed door and stepped up onto a creaking wooden floor.

It was a tiny space, no more that three metres square, with a wide wooden shelf set beneath a dusty window. The shed had a musty smell: a mixture of fertilizer and sacking. Joseph's green rubber boots were set beneath the shelf and alongside them was a tall pile of grey cardboard punnets with tin handles. Lucy counted out eighteen – six for each of them – and placed them on the shelf.

Hanging by a cord from a rusty nail above the shelf was a pair of Joseph's yellow gardening gloves. She idly lifted them down to examine them. They were well-worn and stained green, with the leather of the palms roughened like a suede shoe. She had often seen the old gardener wearing them as he spread layers of grass cuttings onto the compost bins which stood alongside his shed.

For no particular reason other than idle curiosity, she brought one of the gloves up close to her face and inhaled the pungent aroma of leather and freshly-cut grass. She closed her eyes. It was an eerie sensation which she found quite unsettling. She threw the gloves to the floor, picked up the punnets and rushed out of Joseph's shed without even securing the door.

Lucy ran up the grass path towards Sister Beatrice. Placing the punnets on the grass she flung her arms around the novice and started to sob.

'What is it *meine liebchen*? What has upset you? Do you want to take a rest?'

'No, no, I'm fine. I suddenly felt faint inside that shed, that's all. I expect it was the smell of the fertilizer.'

Deciding that they had collected sufficient redcurrants, Sister Beatrice accompanied the girls to the entrance gate. Lucy and Saskia left her and hand in hand walked across to contemplate the Calvary Cross.

The two girls were becoming very close. They slept in adjoining beds, they attended classes together and frequently went off on walks down by the lakeside. Where there were firm pathways they would usually take Nazri as they found his enthusiasm so contagious

After Sunday Mass on the day following the redcurrant picking session they decided to take him to show him one of Lucerne's cultural landmarks: the world-famous KKL Culture & Congress Centre. Strict convent rules forbade them from leaving the grounds, but it was still possible to make out the building's distinctive profile from far off, perched on the very edge of the lake.

Approaching the huge KKL Nazri became very animated, waving his arms excitedly and shouting in Arabic. Docking directly in front of the Congress Centre was a magnificent vintage paddle-steamer, with its tall single funnel belching out smoke as it was gently guided alongside the landing stage, sounding its deep steam horn. This was the 100-year-old *Uri*, oldest of Lake Lucerne's passenger-carrying vessels. Lucy bent forward and whispered to Nazri: 'I think I shall ask Sister Beatrice if she'll take you for a ride on that boat at Easter.' The Libyan boy seemed delighted by the suggestion and clasped Lucy's hand in thanks.

They turned and began to slowly amble back to the convent, with Lake Lucerne's waters gently lapping onto the edge of their path. Letting her Russian friend push Nazri's wheelchair, Lucy hung back in order to listen to the slow rhythmic sound of the tiny wavelets breaking onto the shingle. She slipped into a light reverie. Not painful, like the garden shed experience, but hopeful. There were thoughts of paddling ankle-deep in waters elsewhere and she was in a cave with her friend Anna, searching for buried treasure. Her strange water-filled daydream was broken by Saskia. 'Lucy! Keep up or we'll be late for lunch!'

~ ~ ~ ~ ~

A few weeks before Easter, just as everything was starting to feel spring-like, Sister Serina announced that afternoon classes had been cancelled so that the whole convent could visit the famous 180-year-old *Löwendenkmal*.

After breakfast the youngsters dutifully climbed into the convent's two minibuses, but everyone seemed very much in the dark as to what exactly they were being taken to see. Ever-knowledgeable Anika assured them that it was "all about a huge lion".

Sister Serina had chosen the day of the visit well as there were very few tourists' cars in the car park which served Lucerne's famous parkland monument. The children climbed down from the busses and formed up into a long file to walk through the woods. It took about twenty minutes.

The gravelled footpath curved round to terminate in a small clearing directly in front of a sheer stone cliff, rising up from an oval pool of water. The tranquil pool was ringed by arching trees, creating the effect of a sort of open-air chapel. Sister Serina instructed the party to form a line at the water's edge, facing the cliff.

In the half-gloom, the youngsters could just make out an elongated cave cut deep into the rock face above the waterline. And there, seemingly lying asleep inside the rock cave, was a lion! It was only a carved stone lion, but it was amazingly realistic. 'Who would ever erect such an intricate stone monument, perched above a pool?' Sister Serina asked the children, but everyone just stared ahead in blank amazement.

The young novice explained that back in the 19th century, the townspeople of Lucerne decided that some sort of lasting monument should be erected to commemorate the lives of the hundreds of brave Swiss soldiers who had died in the French Revolution. In particular, the 700 officers, soldiers and mercenaries who had given their lives defending the French King Louis XVI and Queen Marie Antoinette, after they had taken refuge from the rioters in their Tuileries Palace. The sleeping lion in his cave, Sister Serina told her hushed audience, was that monument. After a short silence, followed by a prayer, the novice instructed her charges to walk back to the mini-buses.

Lucy stayed behind, alone at the water's edge. She watched the lion, almost expecting him to raise his head and look at her. But it was the sound of the trickling water, falling from the floor of the lion's cave and dropping into the pool, which sent shudders down her spine. In her mind's eye, she clearly saw another cave – also being gently washed with water – in a hotter climate. And standing beside her was her best friend Anna.

Snuggled up next Saskia at the back of the bus, Lucy quietly sobbed all the way back to the convent.

By the time the two minibuses drove back through the convent gates Lucy had regained her composure. Sister Serina counted all the children and told them that a special early supper was waiting for them in the Refectory. And as they were very tired from the outing, they were to be excused attending *Compline*. The column of children ran to the Refectory.

~ ~ ~ ~ ~

Knowledgeable French Bernadette announced after breakfast one morning, a few days after the visit to the Lion Cave, that Lucerne would shortly be celebrating its famous *Fasnacht* festival, marking the end of winter. Most of the grown-ups of the town would walk around in fancy costumes, she said, wearing strange masks. 'Many are grotesque and very frightening. And after dark there is singing and dancing and much else in the streets' the French girl added with a giggle. As if to confirm Bernadette's colourful description, two days later the Abbess used her sermon at the Sunday service to denounce the festival as a "pagan ritual".

Mother Vanessa's Sunday sermons were nearly always miserable, ending with what she believed was a spiritually-uplifting message to be taken away. But Lucy seldom left the chapel feeling happier than when she had stepped inside, even on a glorious sunny day. For Easter Sunday itself, the Abbess surpassed herself by recounting the most sombre local legend of all: the origin of the name of the snow-capped mountain which Lucy had first glimpsed through her bedroom window in the Sanatorium - Mount Pilatus. This was one of the things Lucy had set eyes on when she first awoke.

The legend, as recounted by the Abbess in a long and rambling sermon, was the depressing (and, thought level-headed Lucy, far-fetched) idea that whenever it rained exceptionally hard in the area, it was a sign that Pontius Pilate was once again washing his hands of the responsibility for sentencing Our Lord to be crucified!

After the service, on their walk by the lakeside with Nazri, Saskia broke the news to a shocked Lucy that she had been told that morning by Mother Vanessa that arrangements had been made for her to return to Moscow.

'For the Easter vacation, you mean?'

'Possibly longer. In fact I may not be returning next term.'

Lucy stopped pushing the wheelchair. The boy looked round with alarm. 'But why can't you come back next term?' pleaded Lucy. Saskia shrugged but gave no reply.

And so it was that, two days later, the two friends said their fond and tearful farewells in the main hall, watched by Sisters Beatrice and Serina. A black Mercedes taxi waited in the drive and all too quickly had whisked little Saskia away, headed for Zurich Airport and thence to Moscow.

In the dormitory before lights out, the talk was of little else but Saskia's abrupt departure from the convent. It was left to all-knowing Anika to join up the dots. Saskia's father, she said, had once served as a senior government official in the Kremlin. He had been put in charge of an inquiry into a banking scandal. It seems he had uncovered evidence of money laundering, involving some high-up government officials.

'They were sending roubles to places like Cyprus and Malta - and even here to Switzerland!' Where all this highly sensitive information originated from was not revealed. 'Then, out of the blue, Saskia's father was arrested and now he's been charged with corruption. I expect that is why the family has sent for her to be returned to Moscow, as there's bound to be a trial.'

Anika's grim summary was greeted with silence. Sister Beatrice wisely judged that it was time to turn out the lights. 'And there's to be no talking tonight,' she cautioned.

~ ~ ~ ~ ~

Lucy continued to take Nazri for his trips along the shoreline to watch the paddle steamers ferrying tourists to and fro from the landing stage alongside the concert hall. Using some new leather driving gloves which his father had bought him to grip the rims of the chair's wheels, the Libyan boy had mastered the art of mounting and descending short flights of steps unaided. But without the effervescent Saskia their lakeside walks weren't the same. She had been like a sister to Lucy – almost a twin sister – and more than a replacement for her lost friend Anna.

At her place at the breakfast table in the Refectory one morning, Lucy found a large yellow envelope, bearing a set of Russian stamps. Inside was a birthday card from Saskia. There was no reference to her father's trial or any news of her returning to Lucerne. A handwritten message beneath the printed greetings simply said: "To dearest Lucy, with all my love on your 7th birthday. Saskia xxx".

VII

Pizzeria Supper

ANDY WILMOT'S PHONE signalled an incoming call from Detective Inspector Tanner. It was more than two weeks since the SIO had given him an update on the long-running saga of the search for his daughter.

'I didn't like to ring you last Friday,' she began apologetically.

'Why, because it was a year since Lucy went missing?'

'Yes.'

'It's OK. I was braced for the worst. I'm just glad that the tabloids didn't go overboard on it. Why do you suppose that was?'

'Hard to say. Probably all this South African World Cup fever. For once, we should be grateful that our gutter Press has a footie fixation, I suppose. I've no doubt MK's *Citizen* will cover it in their next issue. But it'll just be the usual cut-and-paste stuff.'

After a few moments silence, the policewoman said: 'Actually, Andy, I'm ringing to ask a small favour.'

'Ask away.'

'Our Chief Constable retires at the end of the year and once or twice I've hinted that I wouldn't mind having a go for the job.'

'Good for you! So have you put in an application?'

'Not yet. I'm filling the forms in right now. They've got to be handed in at Force HQ by 4 p.m.'

'Cutting it a bit fine aren't you?'

'Well I was rather on the horns of a dilemma until good old Dave thought of a way round the problem. Technically speaking, any Chief Constable applicant must hold the rank of Assistant Chief

Constable, or the equivalent in other forces like Northern Ireland. But Dave says that as I stood in for three months as acting ACC while the chief's second-in-command was off having major surgery, I'm probably eligible. Anyway nothing ventured.'

'Why not? You've got nothing to lose.'

'Andy – I know this is a bit of a cheek – but I was wondering whether I could give you as a reference?'

'Sure.'

'You don't have to write anything about my policing skills. Just a character reference; how long you've known me - that sort of thing.'

'I'd be glad to.'

'Oh thank you so much. You're an angel. You'll probably get all the bumf by the weekend. Just send it straight back to them (there'll be a pre-paid return envelope). The appointment panel's hearing – that's if I get short-listed – is in three weeks time.'

'Well keep me posted on your progress, will you? And good luck!'

~ ~ ~ ~ ~

Andy Wilmot reversed his Mini Cooper into one of the last empty parking bays on central Milton Keynes' Saxon Gate. He looked across at the curious fascia adorning the pizzeria which DI Tanner had nominated as the venue for their Saturday evening supper rendezvous: her 'thank you' to him for providing a character reference for her job application. He was sure she would be regaling him with the details of her appearance before the Chief Constable Appointments Panel.

In raised chrome capitals, set above a green and brown camouflage background, were the words AIR RAID SHELTER. The street window of the restaurant was not only whitewashed, obscuring any view of the interior, but was neatly criss-crossed with a diagonal matrix of brown masking tape. As he crossed the boulevard, he wondered whether he should have brought a tin hat. A quartet of youths kitted out in khaki battle fatigues preceded him inside.

The spacious interior of the pizzeria was every bit as realistic as its street front. The walls were lined with rectangular white glazed tiles (reminiscent of the London Underground during the Blitz), though several areas remained unfinished, revealing bare brickwork. World War Two posters – such as the famous WALLS HAVE EARS warning, and the DIG FOR VICTORY exhortation – were set at angles over the unfinished tile work, illuminated by spotlights simulating wartime anti-aircraft searchlights. The floor was a rugged rough-finished concrete, lit by unshaded light-bulbs hanging from the partially-plastered ceiling.

Slatted timber tables, seating four diners, had unpainted metal-framed garden chairs round each of them. Wartime utility was the watchword and whenever a cooked pizza was ready for collection from the zinc counter in front of the cavernous kitchen, an air raid 'all clear' siren sounded. Despite its sombre theme, the restaurant was buzzing with activity. Andy soon spotted Deborah, seated in a tiny brick-vaulted alcove. He narrowly missed bumping into a petite waitress, clad in a waisted battledress tunic, incongruously set above a tartan mini-skirt.

Complementing her newly-trimmed silver buzz cut, the policewoman was wearing a black lace-trimmed silk camisole, under a black, scallop-edged sleeveless tunic, loosely fastened by a silver ribbon belt. Her gunmetal grey silk slacks were edged with silver ribbon, over black suede pumps with chrome toecaps.

He paused in front of her. 'Well, Mrs Tanner, I must say you look absolutely stunning! Come to think of it, this is only the second time I've ever seen you out of uniform.'

'Why thank you, kind sir. I nearly came dressed in black.'

'Why, who's died?'

'No one. I didn't get the fucking job!'

Hands on hips, Andy stood in front of her dumbfounded. 'Well it certainly couldn't have been anything to do with that glowing reference I sent in'. After a pause, he added: 'Hey let me grab a drink. I'll be right back.' He crossed to the bar, returning with a bottle of Chianti.

'I thought I might as well get a bottle.' Vera Lynn was singing her heart out to the forces. 'Top-up? Right: now tell me all about it. First of all, when was it?'

She held out her half-empty glass for Andy to refill it and then took a long swig. Staring down glumly at a place-mat depicting a Morrison Shelter, she began to fill him in with the details of her interview for the post of Bedfordshire's Chief Constable.

'It was the day before yesterday. In the main council chamber of the Shire Hall. And they – that's the members of the Appointment Panel - were sat in a row, up on the top bench. Five of them. All looking down on the applicants. That was enough to put you off to start with as it felt more like a court of law.'

'So who were they, this five?'

'The chairman was Whitfield-Lewis. He's our new Police and Crime Commissioner. Ineffective little worm. Hardly said a word. Left it to the other four to give little Debs a good mauling, didn't he? He was flanked by our local MP, and the Leader of the County Council, with two formidable women as bookends. One was the new Head of the College of Art; I rather liked her as she was the only one that smiled at me. At the other end was an ugly old trout named Marjorie Fawcett. She's a JP. I've seen her in action in court. A paid-up member of the hang 'em and flog 'em brigade.'

Andy scoffed. 'I think I know the sort; we've got a school governor like her! So how many applicants were there?'

'There was only four of us; me and three blokes. All smarmed up they were: black shiny shoes and Masonic ties, sporting their long-service ribbons and stinking of *Brut*. They all outranked me. Two got interviewed in the morning and I went in to bat first after the lunch break.

'Worst of it was we had been told we'd have to stay on to the end, in order to hear the announcement of the result. So I spent the best part of the day in an over-heated ante-room, reading two-year-old copies of *Country Life*.' She tipped back the last of her wine. 'Cumbria's ACC got the job.'

'Oh Deborah, I'm really sorry for you. Sounds like the odds were stacked against you.'

'You can say that again. Do you know how many female Chief Constables there are in the forty-three English forces?'

'Twelve?'

'Seven, although one's a dyke. One in six. Yet twenty-one per cent of ALL police officers across the force are women. I wonder what your Mrs Pankhurst would think of that for emancipation!' Andy topped her glass up.

Fuelled by the Chianti, Deborah Tanner had now shifted gear into full feminist overdrive. 'In comparison with the armed services, I suppose we're really doing quite well. How many of the 200 serving Major Generals and Brigadiers in the British Army do you suppose are women?'

'Twenty?'

She pointed an index finger towards the table top.

'Ten?'

She smiled and shook her head. 'Two.' Deborah took another long swig. 'Anyway...I was doing reasonably well to start with. Usual predictable questions: crowd control at football matches; anti-terrorist procedures; major incident management; blah-blah-blah. All that sort of thing. 'Then old Trenchard...'

'Who?'

'Sir Brian Trenchard, our MP. He asks me what my views were on "The Black Policemens Association." I politely pointed out to him that the NBPA's correct title is The National Black Police Association. I said that I tended to agree with those who had suggested, at its formation in 1994, that it would prove counter-productive to racial harmony within the force. The berk just pulled a long face. So Nul Points for Debs there.

'Then right out of the blue, Mrs Face-Ache Fawcett MBE bowls me a vicious googly. "And how are you getting on with Orchid?" she asks.' "I believe you are the SIO."'

Andy cut in. 'Orchid?'

'It's our operational name for finding your Lucy. Jeez: the impertinence of the bloody woman! Raising a confidential police investigation at an Appointment Panel. "The inquiry is ongoing, Madam", I tell her all po-faced. I had a shrewd idea that she'd seen that nasty article by Terry Danter in last week's Citizen, asking why there hadn't been any developments in the last twelve months. Then with a conspiratorial side glance at the chairman, she asks: "And how many sightings of the poor little girl have there been, Mrs Tanner?"'

'None to date, Madam, I told her. I looked plaintively at Whitfield-Lewis for some help, but the creep just ignored me. He reminds me of that Len Goodman on Strictly. Little Debs certainly didn't get a ten from Len. Then, as if to twist the knife, her ladyship adds: "Just one final question - if I may, Mr Chairman (fluttering her eyelashes at him like Hyacinth Bouquet). "And is there a Mr Tanner?"'

'What did you say?'

For the first time in the exchange, Deborah gave a huge smile. 'Burnt my boats, didn't I? "Yes, I said, as far as I know, Madam. But I haven't seen him since I showed him the door three years ago. He transferred to Northumbria Constabulary".

'Well of course that was curtains for Debs, wasn't it? Bad enough a bit of skirt having the bare-faced effrontery to compete with three blokes to run the county's force. But a horny middle-aged singleton, lusting after all those new recruits? That would never do.'

Andy could see Deborah was filling up. 'So what did you do when you heard the result?'

'I went home and watched a compilation called *Strictly Bloops*. Restores your self-confidence watching other people trip over.'

He smiled as he refreshed her drink. 'Will you stay in the force?'

'I'm not giving up until we find your Lucy.' She took another swig of the red wine, relieved that the reminiscence was over. 'I tell you Andy: we're going to find her.'

Seeing the young mini-skirted waitress approaching their table, he said: 'Let's order first, shall we? How about two Florentines, on thin pastry bases, with a side order of garlic dough balls?'

'Sounds good to me. I'm famished! And can we have another bottle of Chianti, please?' Deborah asked the waitress.

Al Bowlly had replaced Vera Lynn on the sound system. A tin-hatted lookalike of Sergeant Hodges from *Dad's Army* moved amongst the tables admonishing: 'Get those lights out! Don't you know there's a war on?'

After the wine arrived, Andy asked: 'So how are Dave and Wendy?'

'They're both fine. Dave's only part-time on Orchid now; and my lovely Wendy's applied for the job of PA to the new Chief Constable. She should walk it.'

'So you're down to one-and-a-half. Plus the redoubtable HOLMES.'

'Yup. After a pause, she gave him a nice friendly smile. 'Now tell me about your plans.'

'Well...Doreen and I are definitely going to go our separate ways. She's becoming very frail.' He shook his head. She seems to have aged ten years since Lucy disappeared. Says she can't face going back to work. She's talking about moving to Bristol, to be near her brother. And to cap it all, yesterday she got me to collect a book she'd ordered from our local library. Would you believe: it's called *Messages from Beyond*.'

Mid-way through sipping her wine, Deborah spluttered. ''struth! Madame Arcati arrives in Milton Keynes.'

Andy held up the palms of his hands in mock-surrender. 'I know; I know. Next thing you know we'll be having séances around the kitchen table at Meadowcroft Way.'

'Andy, tell your wife from me she's barking up the wrong tree. We're taken through all this in basic police training. These psychic cranks, with their spiritualist mumbo-jumbo, are attracted to major incidents like murders and abductions – even bullion raids – in the hope of some reflected glory. Of course we're obliged to record their evidence in our MIR logs, but nothing ever comes of it. Remember Peter Sutcliffe, the Yorkshire Ripper? Some Dutch nutter only tried to tell the police that the killer they were looking for was a 27-year-old washing-machine mechanic living in Aberdeen!'

Though Deborah's cautionary advice about clairvoyance was eminently sensible, Andy knew better than to pass it on, given the smouldering resentment which his wife had now built up against the woman detective.

'If I was you, I'd take that book back to the library in the morning.'

'I will.'

'Listen - I'm really sorry about you and Doreen. I've been there. Believe me, separation can be very painful. Tell her she mustn't give up hope. She'll see her Lucy again one day; I'm absolutely certain of it. Will you stay in Milton Keynes?'

'I can't afford to. Flats in Bristol are very pricey and I know Doreen will expect half of what we get for the bungalow if we divorce. I'm thinking of moving back up north. To Durham. I've been offered a job in the university library.'

'Really? Doing what?'

'Setting up their new electronic research archive. It'll only be part-time to start with. It will probably take me some time to wind down all my obligations at the academy. And then we've got to sell the bungalow.'

She reflected as she swirled the red liquid around the bowl of her glass. 'I've never been to Durham.'

'Well, when I'm settled in you must come up and visit me.' He suddenly realised that this was the closest he'd come to making a pass at this attractive young woman.' We could make a weekend of it. Durham Cathedral is magnificent. Ask Dave Williams.'

'I'd like that. But only on one condition.'

'What's that?'

She gave an impish grin. 'Don't book me into the local Travelodge. I'll come and stay with you.'

After paying the bill, Andy escorted Deborah to the door. Billie Holiday was just taking over from Al Bowlly and it was getting pretty noisy inside the Air Raid Shelter pizzeria.

On the street outside a blast of cold wind caught them both by surprise. 'Listen, I don't think I ought to drive, Andy. I'm going to take a taxi.'

'Same for me. I'll pick my car up in the morning. How far away from here do you live? We could share a taxi.'

She nodded at the wide, brightly-lit shopping street that stretched straight ahead. 'Just at the bottom of Saxon Gate. Only about a quarter of a mile.'

'Then why don't I walk you home?'

She clasped his hand tightly. 'I thought you'd never ask!'

VIII

Adoption

SHORTLY BEFORE Christmas 2012, Mother Vanessa announced in the Refectory one morning that she had received an invitation for all members of the convent to attend a concert at the KKL Centre. Lucy and Nazri were thrilled at the thought of seeing the interior of the futuristic building for the first time.

By courtesy of the KKL's management, the Abbess said, the convent had been given complimentary seats in the concert hall's upper balcony, to hear a performance of the Elgar Cello Concerto. The party would be going in a specially-hired coach and the concert was to be followed by a fireworks display over Lake Lucerne.

Everyone dressed up for the occasion, with the Abbess wearing her special ceremonial shawl bearing a pectoral cross woven in gold, its three arms decorated with rubies and a facetted crystal at its centre.

While the convent party filed up the staircases which linked each tier of the hall, Lucy and Nazri rode up in a lift and sat together on the end of a row. Perched high up in the hall's fourth tier, beneath the giant dish-shaped roof, their view down to the semi-circular stage was dizzying.

It was a star-studded occasion, with music by the world-famous Orchestre de la Suisse Romande, from Geneva. But it was the young Chinese woman who played the cello solo, perched on the edge of a small stool, straddling her huge instrument and using dramatic bowing movements, who electrified Lucy. As the audience applauded at the end of the final movement, Lucy clutched Nazri's arm tightly and cried with joy.

The firework display which followed the concert was equally exciting, with colourful multi-layered set-piece displays, one starburst cascading into another, like giant celestial chrysanthemums. Nazri waved his arms in the air jubilantly. There was a brief pause as the sky over Lake Lucerne returned to matt black. A solid boom, which shook the ground, signalled the finale. After a delay of five seconds a huge maroon exploded right above the heads of the crowd, closely followed by four more volleys. The final explosion erupted into a staccato of high-speed bangs, akin to machine-gun fire.

Then silence. The skies above the KKL darkened and the crowd relaxed, realising that the evening's entertainment was at an end. Clutching the handles of Nazri's wheelchair, Lucy saw that the little Libyan boy was bent forwards sobbing, his head buried in his lap and his gloved hands clamped over his ears. Sisters Beatrice and Serina sensibly decided that he should be returned to the convent in a wheelchair-friendly taxi, accompanied by Lucy.

~ ~ ~ ~ ~

Two weeks after the KKL concert, on the day before Lucy's fellow pupils were due to return from Christmas holidays at home with their families, Sister Beatrice told her that they both had to attend an important meeting with the Abbess in the Calefactory after breakfast.

As they descended the stairs together, Lucy noticed that the young novice seemed unusually quiet and thoughtful. The convent clock was striking nine as they walked into the deserted room, taking their places on a bench seat at the side of the big fire. Some minutes passed, with Beatrice giving no hint as to why they had been summoned. She clasped her crucifix with her head bowed in prayer.

After several minutes of silence, the door at the far end opened and the Abbess entered, followed by a stocky man wearing a black jacket, dark pinstriped trousers and crisp white shirt. His necktie, which he kept nervously adjusting, was a strange design of zigzag red lines over a blue background. His clean-cut complexion was almost as dark-skinned as Nazri's and his gold-rimmed glasses added a discomfiting look to his hooded eyes. Having studied many pictures in the finishing school's etiquette books, Lucy decided that the stranger's appearance was not unlike that of a butler.

Mother Vanessa took a seat opposite, beside her visitor. 'As I am sure Sister Beatrice will have explained to you, Lucy,' she began formally, 'this convent prides itself in also being an orphanage. Several of our pupils – Bernadette in your dormitory, for example, and two of the boys in Leo – have no families. In exceptional cases – once their education with us has been completed - we are sometimes able to give these unfortunate children new homes with adoptive parents, often in their country of origin. It is a Christian achievement of which we are very proud.' She half-turned towards the stranger who nodded his approval.

'I am pleased to be able to tell you that the gentleman seated beside me has expressed a willingness to commence adoption procedures, should you agree, for you to live in England once your education here in Lucerne is completed. This is Mr Aamir Kashani and he lives in London.' Without pausing to hear Lucy's response to this earth-shattering news, the Abbess turned to the silent visitor to address them.

'Thank you Mother Vanessa.' The man suddenly seemed tongue-tied and shifted uncomfortably on the bench. He adjusted his tie. 'As the Abbess has told you, I live in London. I am a businessman, specialising in the importation of rare carpets and rugs from Iraq and Afghanistan.' He made a nervous cough and took out a silk pocket handkerchief, which he dabbed delicately against the side of his mouth.

'Three years ago my wife and I lost our daughter to a rare and incurable cancer. It was a tremendous blow to us both. But now I am determined to move forwards again. For this reason I recently made contact with the convent, in the hope that it might be able to assist me with my adoption endeavours.' For the first time the man looked directly at Lucy. 'I would so very much like to be able to offer a new home to a young person like you.'

There was silence in the room. Beatrice looked at Lucy, taking her hand and nodding gently, indicating that some form of polite response would be appropriate. The Abbess glared impatiently at the girl. 'Thank you for your kind offer,' said Lucy. That was all.

~ ~ ~ ~ ~

The following day was Sunday which meant two things: a long service in the chapel, culminating in one of Mother Vanessa's moralistic diatribes, followed by a peaceful walk beside Lake Lucerne with Nazri. During the sermon Lucy determined to share her problem with the boy.

Nazri took no time at all in reaching a conclusion. 'Go for it, Lucy!'

'Really? You think so?'

'Sure. You've got nothing to lose – and probably lots to gain. If it was me - say I'd lost both my parents in the Tripoli bombing – I'd certainly want to start a new life. Somewhere fresh. London sounds terrific!'

So it was that in the dormitory that evening, Lucy confided to Beatrice her willingness to accept Mr Kashani's offer. 'Then I shall say a special prayer for you tonight' said the novice.

But despite little Nazri's enthusiasm, Lucy still had serious misgivings. It seemed to her especially cruel that ever time she formed a close friendship – Anna (of whom she only had clouded memories), Saskia, Nazri, Beatrice – they were taken away from her.

~ ~ ~ ~ ~

It wasn't until after Easter that Lucy learned that she had been recommended for transfer to the convent's highly-regarded pre-finishing school. She had heard virtually nothing about the adoption, though Beatrice had assured her that such arrangements often took as long as a year to complete.

Lucy was rather surprised that the Brat Pack had also been chosen for transfer, though cynical Anika was quite sure that "large sums of money probably changed hands". None of the finishing school's teaching staff were nuns, though as she was to remain in Pius Dormitory, Lucy would not lose contact with her 'unofficial older sister' Beatrice, and lakeside walks with Nazri after the Sunday service would still be possible. Attendance at both *Prime* and *Compline* remained obligatory.

Lucy was soon to discover that "Pre-finish" (as it came to be known by its pupils) was a much more enjoyable experience than the dull and repetitive religious and science lessons which she had been forced to endure.

Cookery turned out to be her favourite class and she soon excelled with many of the most complex recipes. Almond custard-filled profiteroles became her speciality. But the finer points of such things as table settings and the use of the correct cutlery, she found rather pointless.

She enjoyed needlework and flower arranging, but found etiquette and deportment tiresome. However, this latter category produced one moment of hilarity amongst the feisty Brat Pack when their Italian teacher *Signorita* Vincenzi demonstrated the pitfalls of not performing the 'Cambridge Cross'. This, she explained, involved learning how to sit in "a ladylike manner", crossing ones legs between knee and ankle, to prevent young men from looking up your skirt.

According to all-knowing Anika, the glamorous *Signorita* had once been on the catwalk as a fashion model, though her flamboyant dress sense was not appreciated by the Abbess. She took particular exception to her arriving for Sunday Mass wearing white-rimmed sunglasses, body-hugging pencil skirts and stilettos.

The days in Pre-finish fairly flew by and very soon most of the convent's pupils had headed for their long summer holidays at home with their families. Lucy, Anika and the four Kuwaiti girls were the only ones who didn't go home.

On her 9th birthday a card arrived from London – postmarked Barbican EC2 – with a courteous message signed by Aamir Kashani, enclosing a 50 Euro note. There was still no news from Moscow.

~ ~ ~ ~ ~

Lucy wasn't made party to the lengthy adoption process, learning what little she could from whispered messages from Sister Beatrice, usually at bedtime. Nazri continued to give his enthusiastic support for the idea of moving to London and after one visit from his parents, enthused about Lucy's possible new home in the Barbican. 'My Dad says it's a very swanky development of luxury apartments in the City of London. And guess what?'

'Tell me.'

'He says it's even got its own concert hall and a school of music, where local young people I taught to play instruments!'

'Like the cello?'

'Yup, even the cello.'

~ ~ ~ ~ ~

Nine months after first being given the opportunity to move to England - in the Abbess's rather terse *fait accompli*, Lucy heard that she would be leaving Lucerne at the end of the winter term and flying to London with the mysterious Mr Kashani. Beatrice explained that the delay had been caused by the adoption paperwork between England and Switzerland.

Two nights before she was due to leave Lucerne, Lucy had a disturbing nightmare. She dreamed she was standing at the water's edge of a tiny cove, hand in hand with a freckle-faced girl who was dressed as a pirate, gazing wistfully into the entrance of a dark cave.

The other girl wanted to wade through the shallows to go into the cave to explore inside. But cautious Lucy held back and turned to see if there were any grownups watching. Above them, on the cliff's edge directly overlooking the cove, a dark-skinned man in a black jacket and black pinstriped trousers watched the pair. The nightmare ended abruptly and Lucy sat up in bed.

She didn't manage to get properly back to sleep again and was wide awake when the bell tolled for *Prime*. After breakfast, there was a half-hour to spare before Lucy's final cookery session. She felt a need to discuss her dream with Beatrice, whom she knew would be in her cell. The corridor where the nuns lived was strictly out of bounds to all pupils.

After the mass exodus from the Refectory, Lucy waited about ten minutes before venturing out. She went first to the octagonal hall with its lovely lavender scent, then into the narrow arched passageway where the nuns' cells were located.

The corridor was dimly lit by small candles, set in niches along one wall. Studded wooden doors lined the other wall. At the far end, lit by a cluster of night lights was an icon of a bejewelled Madonna. Lucy tiptoed along the corridor, scared that one of the older nuns – from the Abbess's cabal - might suddenly appear.

The cell doors were marked with small cards. Beatrice's was at the far end next to the icon. Lucy nervously tapped on the door then, without waiting for a response, lifted the latch and went in.

Beatrice was sitting at a small desk reading her Bible. The novice turned and looked up with alarm. 'Lucy, my dear, what is it?' Lucy quietly closed the door and sat down on the edge of the narrow bunk bed.

'Last night I had a scary dream. But I didn't want to tell you about it in the dormitory in front of the others.' The girl then carefully recounted her vision. 'So is it God giving me a warning? Is he telling me not to go to London with that man?'

Beatrice reached out to Lucy and clasped both her hands. 'It was just a dream, dear.' She spoke quietly. 'Your brain was probably overworked from your day's studies. And the excitement about your journey to London. You mustn't read anything more significant into it.'

'But I shall be losing all my friends like Nazri and Anika and Bernadette. And you.'

'We can write.'

'Could you come and visit me in London, perhaps?'

There was a long pause while the novice tried to form a polite response. 'I very much doubt it, my child. You see we nuns are committed to living here, to be close to God. Even Mother Superior seldom travels far and then it is always on convent business. Nuns and novices don't have holidays, I'm afraid.' The whispered conversation was cut short by the tolling of the bell for the *Terce* service. The latch on an adjoining cell door clicked, followed by several others. Beatrice held a finger to her lips and the two looked at each other nervously in silence.

After the echoing footfalls of the departing nuns had subsided, the novice opened her cell door and beckoned Lucy to slip out. Moments later she walked calmly towards the morning service in the convent chapel.

~ ~ ~ ~ ~

On the day of her departure from the convent, Lucy's farewells were many and invariably tearful. Hardest of all was to say goodbye to the stalwart Beatrice, who had proved to be such a comfort to the young woman from the first moment that she opened her eyes in that pristine white room in the sanatorium. The hugged each other closely.

Sister Beatrice pressed a small box wrapped in pink tissue paper into Lucy's hand. 'Now promise me, *meine liebchen*, that you won't open it until you are on the plane?'

'I promise.'

Aamir Kashani arrived promptly at noon, to be greeted by the Abbess. He shook her hand and handed her a large brown envelope. Beatrice helped to load Lucy's luggage into the boot of the big Mercedes, watched by a gaggle of her best friends, including a proud Nazri, dressed in a new blue Superman T-shirt. Then there was one final hug from Sister Beatrice before she climbed into the car, clutching her gift. As the limousine glided down the convent's gravel drive, Lucy glanced from a side window to see the sombre Cross of Calvary for the last time.

The illuminated sign above the airport's main entrance read: FLUGHAFEN ZURICH. The vast interior was all glass and stainless steel, made extra-bright by huge glass-beaded chandeliers hanging from the roof.

~ ~ ~ ~ ~

Although she believed it to be the first time that she had ever set foot inside an airport building, there were things there that seemed eerily familiar to Lucy. The rattle of luggage trolleys, continually criss-crossing the busy departures hall; strange disembodied voices, announcing - in many languages – flight numbers and times and destinations; and the tall haughty woman, with a blue turban headdress, who unsmilingly checked their flight tickets and passports.

The airline they were flying with was called Swiss International. Once inside its gloriously comfortable first class cabin, Kashani and Lucy settled down into big squishy black leather seats. Another woman with a blue turban offered Lucy a sucking sweet – though this one did smile.

As the white and silver aeroplane taxied ready for its take-off, the deafening noise of its powerful jet engines made the young girl certain that she had heard such a sound before, somewhere in the dim and distant past.

After take-off, she took Sister Beatrice's gift from her shoulder bag and removed its tissue wrapping. It was a CD recording of Jacqueline du Pré performing the Elgar Cello Concerto, with a lovely picture of her on the box.

Kashani pulled a pale blue carrier bag from his bag and dropped it in Lucy's lap. 'A small gift for you to use in London.' was all he said. The bag was marked ASPREY. For sheer ostentation, Kashani's gift outshone the novice's CD. Inside the bag Lucy found an iPhone in a pink suede wallet, its cover monogrammed in gold with the letters LK. Inside the silk-lined pouch, a vanity mirror faced the smart phone's screen.

The meal which the friendly stewardess served them soon made Lucy sleepy, and it wasn't until she heard an announcement that they would shortly be landing at London Heathrow, that she realised that her journey to England was almost complete. Her father had barely addressed a single word to her during the two-hour flight, remaining engrossed in a pink newspaper called *Financial Times*.

After the plane had taxied to a halt in front of a brightly-lit terminal building, Lucy followed Kashani out through the connecting sky-bridge and along interminable corridors until they reached a silent queue of people of all nationalities waiting to have their passports checked. Then through more corridors and into a huge hall, where throngs stood behind a rope barrier holding aloft signs which said things like: THOMAS COOK, SKY TOURS and ALL SEASONS TRAVEL.

Grasping her shoulder, her father guided her towards a tall man in a dark grey uniform, wearing a peaked cap. In one gloved hand he held a sign saying: KASHANI. This, she was to discover, was Roland the chauffeur. Pushing their luggage on a trolley, he led them to an underground car park. Then they climbed inside yet another shiny black limousine. The chauffeur wrapped a lovely lambswool rug around Lucy's legs, while her father sat in the front beside the driver. She was soon fast asleep again.

The drive to the capital took less than two hours. Lucy awoke as they reached the outskirts of the City of London and was stunned by the sheer scale of the buildings all around her. She had never seen anything as big as these – with the possible exception of the KKL.

The car entered a long brightly-lit traffic tunnel. At the far end Roland slowed the pace, then expertly reversed the long car into a space between two delivery vans. 'Thank you Roland', said Kashani, opening the rear door for Lucy. 'Be sure to collect me at 8.30 a.m. tomorrow, as usual. We can unload Lucy's luggage then.' He took out their hand luggage. 'Welcome to your new home in the Barbican, my dear.' Roland drove away.

Aamir Kashani looked proudly skywards. 'This building is called Churchill Tower, named after the famous British Prime Minister.' Lucy recalled the name from a history lesson.

Her new home looked rather daunting and unfriendly. Built entirely of a sort of rugged concrete, it was well over of forty storeys high. Each floor was identical, punctuated by the same number of windows. And sticking out at each level – eerily silhouetted by the night sky – were ugly horn-shaped projections, which she was later to discover were the balconies of each apartment.

The man and the young girl walked into the deserted lobby of Churchill Tower. Kashani nodded to the Fijian security guard but didn't address him. Malcolm X had often noted that this aloof and unfriendly businessman always wore the regimental tie of The Royal Artillery. He was not to know that Kashani had never even served in the army.

They rode up in the cramped elevator, halting at the 37th floor. With a flourish, Aamir Kashani opened the front door of his apartment with a latch key attached to a gold chain and ushered Lucy into a small entrance hall, setting down their bags.

'Now unless you would like anything to eat or drink, I suggest we go to bed as I imagine you must be very tired after that long journey. You will find the bathroom is at the far end of the corridor on the right and your bedroom is opposite. Audrey, our housekeeper, will be here promptly at eight tomorrow morning and I shall leave her a note to bring you your breakfast on a tray. When you awake I shall probably have left for work.' He picked up the girl's hand luggage and gave a smile. 'Now let me show you to your bedroom.'

~ ~ ~ ~ ~

It was 9.30am when Lucy was woken by bright shafts of sunlight falling onto her bed. A plump black lady in a blue overall was pulling back the curtains. She turned and gave Lucy a lovely beaming smile.

'Good morning! I'm Audrey, your Dad's housekeeper. He left me a note to say that you would probably like a soft-boiled egg for breakfast.' She placed a tray on Lucy's lap as she sat up. 'There's bread and butter soldiers too. And some marmalade. Just call if you need anything.'

'Thank you, Audrey,' said Lucy as the elderly lady waddled out.

Lucy washed and dressed after her breakfast, eager to explore her new surroundings. Audrey was in the kitchen putting some china away. 'I don't expect Mr Kashani will be back until late tonight.

After work he often goes to his club. So before I go this evening, what shall I get you for your supper?'

'Spaghetti on toast would be nice' answered Lucy.

'Right you are.' The woman began filling a small watering can. 'Now I must go out and water them plants on the balcony before the sun gets up.'

Lucy wandered into the big sitting room which adjoined the kitchen. Through the wide picture window she watched Audrey lovingly attend to a large collection of flowering plants and two lofty canes of semi-ripe tomatoes.

Beyond the balcony rail the view across London was dizzying. St Paul's Cathedral's famous dome was in the centre, surrounded by countless huge office towers. Immediately below, the people walking across the broad paved square looked like ants. There was also a huge ornamental pool with fountains playing. As Audrey stepped back into the kitchen Lucy asked: 'Would it be all right if I went and explored downstairs, after I'm dressed?'

'I'm afraid not, my lovely. Your Dad gave strict instructions that you weren't to go out alone. You'll have to talk to him about it at breakfast tomorrow. And he's also told me that you shouldn't go into his study.'

'Why is that?'

'Search me, darling. Unless it's on account of all them antique rugs he's got in there. He won't even let me hoover them.'

~ ~ ~ ~ ~

Although she had been enrolled in a school in north London, Lucy learned that there was still two weeks before the start of the new term. Being prevented from exploring the Barbican in the way she had enjoyed wandering along the edge of Lake Lucerne, the days seemed awfully long. One afternoon Lucy and Audrey decided to settle down to a quiet game of Scrabble in Kashani's study.

The word game was not the housekeeper's favourite pastime, but she felt it helped to while away the hours of solitary boredom that her young charge had to suffer, incarcerated in Churchill Tower. For Lucy, these occasional games were a subtle way of enlarging Audrey's vocabulary.

The housekeeper laid down tiles spelling the word 'FORTENT'.

'No such word,' shouted Lucy, reaching for her iPhone.

'Oh yes there is. Back home in Cuba the Santeros used it all the time. It's a bad warning sign.'

The girl showed the housekeeper the screen. It read: "PORTENT: A sign or warning that a momentous or calamitous event is likely to happen". 'I'll let you have 'tent' though. That's four.'

'Well that was a bit of a damp squid, wasn't it?' observed Audrey grumpily.

They were both giggling when the study door swung open to reveal Lucy's stern-faced father, who had returned unexpectedly early.

'I shall take tea in the salon, thank you Audrey.' The players sheepishly abandoned their game, hastily packing it away in its box. Audrey crept out to prepare her employer's tea.

Alone in the sitting room, Lucy watched her father drink his tea in silence, gazing out of the window at a sun-lit St Paul's. It was now nearly two months since he had brought Lucy back from Lucerne. And yet they seemed no closer. 'I think it would be best if you let the housekeeper perform the duties she is paid for,' he announced imperiously.

'I'm very fond of Audrey, father. Our Scrabble games help her to learn new English words. And they're fun too.'

'Nevertheless, Lucy, it is my fervent wish that you should desist from such frivolities. I'm sure you have work to prepare for the first term at your new school.' He placed his cup on the tea trolley and walked out of the room. The 'discussion' had been ended peremptorily, in much the same way as Lucy's two meetings with the Abbess.

~ ~ ~ ~ ~

The early days of their relationship were tense and sometimes acrimonious. Confusingly for Lucy, the terms Father, Step-father and Adoptive Father seemed to be interchangeable since her arrival in the Barbican. In Lucerne, Sister Beatrice had explained that as a result of the adoption process Aamir Kashani was officially Lucy's Adoptive Father. Audrey simply regarded him as the girl's Dad.

Lucy had been enrolled at St Broderick's, a multi-faith school in the borough closest to Kashani's carpet warehouse. Each day Roland would take her to school (after dropping off his employer) and collect her in the afternoon. But being driven to and from school in a chauffeur-driven limo did little to assist the young woman's hopes of 'bonding' with her new schoolmates. 'At least at Lake Lucerne we were all equal' Lucy mused to herself.

St Broderick's had pupils from Italy, Spain and Portugal, as well as a large Asian contingent. Without exception, all the Asian girls wore the hijab. Replacing Lucerne's notorious Kuwaiti Brat Pack, St Broderick's had a no-nonsense gang of four English girls from the Angel, Islington.

Lucy was determined to excel at St Broderick's as her father had hinted that he would make an application for her to enrol at the nearby Guildhall School of Music. She had already started scouring the internet in the hope of finding a second hand cello on e-Bay.

Lucy's end-of-term reports were very encouraging, though no further mention was made about the music school. Twice she hinted to her father that she would so like to go to a live performance at the Barbican Arts Centre. He invariably pleaded that it was 'pressure of work' that prevented him from being home in time to attend a concert. And he could certainly not countenance a ten-year-old girl going to a public concert unescorted.

Her sole relief on these solitary evenings was to listen to her recording of the cello concerto, often sitting on the wide windowsill in the sitting room, gazing at the flood-lit dome of St Paul's and letting her beloved Jackie provide feelings of peace and tranquillity, with wistful remembrances of times with Beatrice returning whenever the slow movement played.

~ ~ ~ ~ ~

For her first Christmas in London Lucy had sent cards to all her friends who she knew were still at the convent, as well as an especially chatty one to Sister Beatrice.

A few days into New Year she was thrilled to receive an envelope bearing Swiss stamps. In it was a card from her lovely Nazri, accompanied by a photo. This showed him sitting in his wheelchair on the steamer landing stage in front of the KKL hall. The wheels of his chair now sported jaunty yellow emojis. He was flanked by his proud parents and a smiling Sister Beatrice. The message on the card included the amazing news that he had been selected to compete in the 200 metre wheelchair event of the World Paralympics Junior Championships, which were due to be held in the spring in Switzerland. There was no card from Moscow.

Though the significance of the smart residential estate's name had initially been lost on the newcomer, a history lesson at school one day highlighted its origins. A barbican, Lucy learned, was originally a medieval fortified gateway or citadel. So she had simply moved from one secure, cloistered environment – the Convent of the Blessed Sisters of the Sacred Order of the Immaculate Conception – to another, where some of the wealthiest people in London lived in privileged isolation. In Lucerne, her closest adult companion had been Sister Beatrice. In the City of London Roland was now her watchful 'minder'.

After several months of solitary confinement, Lucy devised an ingenious 'escape route', enabling her to slip away from 'The Tower' (as she had now come to regard it). With Audrey's collusion she would travel down in the block's goods lift (normally reserved for refuse collections) to the basement service area, returning by the same route, and be let back in by the Cuban housekeeper, thus evading detection by Malcolm X.

Kashani's staff: put-upon Audrey, servile Roland and silent Tomas - the Serbian who worked at the warehouse – were invariably treated, Lucy decided, like the underlings of a feudal lord. With Tomas she especially harboured grave concerns. For while he always addressed her respectfully whenever she visited her father's warehouse, the youth would often stare at her blankly, as if he knew something that troubled him.

The intricacies of her father's importation business were another thing which troubled the ever-watchful Lucy. Clearly he had an unrivalled knowledge of oriental carpets – that much was clear from the frequent phone calls he made and received when at home. But where some of the smaller items – his beloved Mesopotamian antiquities – went to was a mystery. Similarly puzzling for the girl were Kashani's abrupt and unannounced after-supper departures (usually preceded by a telephone call from someone called Carla). They were invariably a sign that he wouldn't return until well after Lucy had gone to bed. Sometimes not until the following morning.

At the Barbican, pride of place on the window shelf in the sitting room had always been a small statuette of a warrior, holding a long bow and dressed in an intricate suit of armour. Audrey was forbidden to dust it. One weekend it vanished. But when Lucy asked why it had been moved, her father simply replied that it had been "loaned to a collector for appraisal". It never reappeared.

IX

Revelation

AMIR KASHANI and his adopted daughter sat in silence in the sitting room of the Barbican apartment.

In the corner the television picture showed the all-too familiar sight of cricketers leaving the field of play because of rain and climbing the steps into the Oval pavilion. In the corner, Lucy was absorbed by one of her *Teen Romance* magazines.

Geoffrey Boycott's distinctive Yorkshire voice boomed out. "Eeeeee, I'll go to the foot of our stairs. They're only coming off. I don't BELIEVE it!"

"Steady on Geoffrey, old bean. It is raining, you know."

"That's not rain. Come on - that's not RAIN! That wouldn't even make a puddle. My Mum used to 'ang 'er washing out in our back yard when it was coming down 'eavier than that. Won't last two minutes, mark my words."

At this point, Kashani switched the TV's sound off by the remote control to take a mobile phone call.

'Mr Kashani? Good afternoon. Deirdre Remington at Bath Square.'

'Good afternoon, Miss Remington. What can I do for you?'

'Well I think I may have a buyer for the large antique rug you put in our show flat.'

'Really? The Oushak?'

'Yes. Unfortunately, the client is saying it's not big enough. He wants to know if you have a larger one, in the same colours and design.'

'I'll have to check, Miss Remington. Can I get back to you?'

'Of course. I'll be here in the office until six this evening.'

Kashani immediately rang his Shoreditch warehouse to check the stock with his assistant, Tomas, where the young Serbian was in the basement, preparing to unpack a new consignment.

'You know the big Anatolian Oushak we put into that show flat in Chelsea? Remind me of its dimensions?'

'Just let me get it up on the system, Sir' the assistant replied. Then, after a pause: 'Five metres by four'.

'Do we have anything of the same provenance bigger than that?'

'I very much doubt it, Mr Kashani, but just let me check.' After another pause: 'I'm afraid not, Sir. That's one of the biggest pieces we've ever had. I remember it only just fitted into the van when we took it over to Chelsea.'

'Mark it "Under Offer" on the system, will you Tomas? By the way, I'm going to the Oval Test Match tomorrow. I'll ring you in the lunch interval.'

'Very good, Sir.'

Kashani quickly rang the estate agent to break the news to her that there were no larger Oushaks available. 'I'm extremely sorry, Miss Remington. Perhaps you could explain to your client that these are all antique pieces – that one is 19th century - not mass-produced broadloom carpets. Twenty square metres is big for a hand-woven tribal piece.'

'I appreciate that. Would you be willing to speak to him yourself, Mr Kashani as you know so much more about these carpets? I know he is anxious to settle the matter quickly as he has to fly back to the Middle East tomorrow.'

'Certainly. I'd be happy to meet him in the show flat this evening, if you wish.'

'Shall we say 6.15? I don't mind staying on to make the introductions.'

'Fine. I'll be at Bath Square at 6.15 sharp.'

Knowing that his driver was out on an errand, the carpet dealer instructed his housekeeper to ring down to reception for a taxi.

Lucy looked up from her magazine as Kashani headed for the hallway. 'Audrey will get your supper, my dear. Don't wait up for me. I'll probably call in at my club after I've finished my business meeting in Chelsea.'

The cross-London taxi run was the usual stop-start procession for a typical rain-sodden mid-week rush hour. Mercifully, the driver made no attempt to engage his fare in conversation, as he was absorbed by the commentary of a football match being broadcast from Madrid. They made it to Bath Square in Chelsea with five minutes to spare.

The huge floodlit entrance portico of the neo-classical building looked more like a New England courthouse than the former municipal library which had been converted into a block of luxury apartments. A top-hatted commissionaire greeted him on the entrance steps. 'Aamir Kashani to see Miss Remington. She's expecting me.'

The man gave him a salute with a gloved hand and pulled one of the huge bronze doors open. 'Of course, Mr Kashani. She's waiting for you in the show flat. Please take the lift to the sixth floor.'

The transformation of the former library had retained the grandiose proportions and decorations beloved of the Victorian benefactors who built so many English town halls, art galleries and libraries. Even the library's opening date was picked out in gilded numerals in the centre of chequerboard floor of the octagonal entrance hall. Kashani rode up in the lift.

The mahogany-panelled door to the show flat was ajar, with a trim-figured Deirdre Remington standing on guard inside.

'Thank you so much for coming over at such short notice, Mr Kashani,' she gushed in a cultured Roedean voice. As they approached the apartment's huge living area, she shifted to a conspiratorial

whisper: 'I should perhaps warn you that His Highness can be...
shall we say... a little demanding.'

Kashani nodded. That was all. There was no time for the young
woman to elaborate, or for the carpet dealer to cross-examine her.
They had reached a wide entrance arch, connecting the long hallway
to the apartment's principal living space, whose double doors were
swung open.

The cavernous room had all the *finesse* of a departures hall in
an airport terminal. There were three eight-seater sofas - all with
a minimum of sixteen scatter cushions – flanked by low, glass-
topped side tables; and a wide coal-effect fire in the centre of a long
limestone fireplace. Above it hung a huge gold-framed architectural
perspective of the proposed $400M National Museum of Quatar at
Doha. To an architectural purist such as Aamir Kashani (who had
a Palladio engraving hanging in his bathroom), the opulent design
looked like nothing more than a stack of giant white saucers.

Centre stage, on a highly-polished oak parquet floor (on which
two Arab men in white robes were standing), was Aamir Kashani's
magnificent Anatolian carpet. Edged by a border of vivid gold and
emerald green, its central field comprised a geometric grid of six-
pointed stars, set on a background of amber and iridescent blue.

'May I introduce Prince Fahad and his equerry?' said Deirdre. 'Mr
Aamir Kashani. Mr Kashani has kindly come over to explain to your
Royal Highness that the carpet on which you are standing is the
largest in his extensive collection. We at Bradmans, have dealt with
Mr Kashani for a number of years, and consider him to be London's
foremost expert in oriental carpets and rugs.'

After this effusive introduction, Deirdre Remington took two
paces back, cocking her head to one side, as if inviting Kashani to
open the bidding. He gave a deferential nod to the taller of the two
Arabs.

'Before coming over here tonight, I checked the stock we hold here in London. Of this particular design and colour scheme, it is the largest available. We could certainly try to seek a larger piece for you, but it would take several months.' It was classic Kashani bluster.

The taller man snapped something in Arabic. 'His Royal Highness says it is out of the question. We must return to Riyadh tomorrow,' the equerry translated.

'As I explained to Miss Remington, these are hand-woven tribal pieces. A similar one to this recently sold at Sotheby's in New York for $30,000.'

The tall Arab looked down irritably at his equerry, as if silently urging him to continue the negotiations.

'His Royal Highness has today instructed the developers to re-lay the floor of the penthouse apartment he is purchasing. They will be removing the oak wood block floor in order to install electric underfloor heating. Then replacing it with marble.'

'Marble?' queried Kashani. 'What colour?'

'White,' answered the factotum. 'It will be brought over from our kingdom.' He offered Kashani a small square sample, the size of a beer mat. The carpet dealer slowly shook his head with disbelief as he fingered the tile – a reaction which was lost on the haughty Saudis, but which didn't slip under Deirdre Remington's radar.

Ever-tactful (and protective of a potential sale) the young woman told Kashani: 'I think what His Royal Highness is striving for is a blend of materials: the primitive style of the Anatolian weaving, contrasted with the modern day splendour of Arabian marble.' She fluttered her eyelashes at the equerry.

'Precisely, Miss Remington: You have so well encapsulated His Royal Highness's thoughts.' Despite Kashani's prolonged scowl, the saleswoman breathed a sigh of relief.

He realised that it was pointless to resist such pigheaded stubbornness. Glancing down at his Oushak, he said: 'Well there it is, gentlemen. I am extremely sorry, but this is the largest piece – of this particular provenance – that I can offer you. I very much doubt whether there is anyone else in London who can help you.' Turning to Deirdre, he added: 'Indeed, if I knew of a source, I would gladly direct you there.' The two Arabs remained mute. It was, in effect, a graceful 'take it or leave it' offer from the shrewd carpet merchant.

The equerry spoke next. 'And the price? Pray remind His Royal Highness of the price for this particular item.'

'£20,000.'

Sensing that this was stalemate and that neither side was prepared to give ground, Deirdre Remington tactfully brought the short visit to a close. Looking imploringly at the Arab prince, she said: 'I know Mr Kashani has to get back to the Barbican. Can I leave you both to communicate by text messages later, as I shall need to tell our builders what your decision is in the morning.' The prince nodded, as Kashani handed the equerry a business card bearing his personal mobile phone number.

~ ~ ~ ~ ~

In the Barbican, Lucy was struggling with her holiday project. 'Audrey – what's the capital of Botswana?'

'Search me, darling. I've never managed to master all them new African countries. Some of them even has different names from when I was at school in Havana. Look it up in your Dad's *World Atlas*, why don't you? It's in his study. It isn't locked. Or else you could Google it.'

From her pre-Googling days in the convent, Lucy remembered the delights of studying maps of foreign countries. She walked down the hall to her father's inner sanctum, a space from which she was officially excluded. Along the polished windowsill which ran the full width of the room, were some of Kashani's prize antiquities – pieces which he was loath to put on the market, not only because of their rarity, but also because of their true provenance. A blue and green Kazak runner ran beneath the shelving.

Under the window shelf were two rows of reference books, mainly dealing with oriental carpets and rugs. She pulled out *The Times World Atlas* and had soon solved her African problem. Replacing the volume in its correct place on the lower shelf, she noticed the bright orange spines of a dozen or so magazines, all entitled *Semi-Quaver*, sandwiched between two sets of *National Geographic*. She pulled out a random copy of *Semi-Quaver*, expecting to find it was about music or musicians. But she was to be disappointed. Describing itself as "a lifestyle publication for the discerning," it was heavy with adverts for international properties, luxury holiday resorts and ocean-going yachts.

As she slid the glossy magazine back into place, she noticed that one of the adjoining issues had a yellow Post-it marker sticking out at the top. She took the marked copy out and opened it, to find a two-page spread entitled 'The Malaga Mystery'. Intrigued by the title, she took it across to her father's desk and sat down to read it.

Beneath the headline, a strapline summarised the article's contents: "Police in Britain and Spain continue to be baffled by the disappearance, from a luxury holiday resort in Andalusia, of six-year-old Lucy Wilmot. The case remains open but unsolved." The article had a number of colour photographs, including an aerial photo of a small seaside cove. Another showed a group of three adults and two young girls, seated at a table in sunshine in front of a pool with a Greek statue at its centre. At the end of the text was a picture of a tall Victorian house. Running across the top of the article were reproductions of some of the original newspaper headlines which had first announced the girl's disappearance.

Lucy began to read the story of a little girl who disappeared one night from a Spanish holiday complex where she had been staying with her parents. The lost girl's name was Lucy. The quoted comments of the British police implied that, though they were still regarding it as a crime of abduction, not a shred of evidence had turned up as to the girl's whereabouts.

The *Semi-Quaver* article ended on a rather sad note. "Mrs Doreen Wilmot, the missing girl's mother, suffered a nervous breakdown shortly after the tragedy and subsequently separated from her husband. She now lives in seclusion in a residential care home in Bristol. She declined to be interviewed for this article." The caption below the picture of an old house at the foot of the page read: "Mrs Wilmot's care home in Clifton, Bristol."

Lucy took out her smart phone and set it on picture-taking mode. After photographing the double-page spread, she returned the magazine to its correct position on the bookshelf, carefully re-inserting the Post-it marker. She heard Audrey call out: 'I shouldn't be too long in there, my lovely; just in case your Dad comes home unexpectedly.'

Puzzled by the magazine's revelations, Lucy crossed to the kitchen. The buxom housekeeper was kneeling on the floor humming to herself, wearing a blue cotton overall and wiping down the inner lining of the fridge. Standing up to admire the job, she peeled off her rubber gloves and observed: "That should pass mustard."

'Audrey?'

'Yes, darling?'

'I want to pop down to the newsagent outside the station to see if the new issue of *Teen Romance* has arrived. Will you be here to let me in?'

'Of course, but try to be back before six would you, my lovely? I want to call in at a charity shop in Smithfield on my way home. They've got one of them transvestite radios in the window and I thought I'd get it for my Wesley so's he can listen to the cricket when he's sat in the garden. He used to play, you know? For the famous Shannon Club in Trinidad. Opened the batting once with Wilton St Hill, he did.'

'You don't say. Right, I'll make sure I'm back by 5.45 at the latest.' Lucy donned a fleecy jacket from the hall, pulled the apartment door to and descended in the goods lift to the basement car park.

As she crossed the cobbled plaza in front of Churchill Tower, the vivid images triggered by the article in the lifestyle magazine kept resonating uncomfortably. Much of it seemed so familiar to her: the appearance of the Spanish holiday resort's terrace and pool and the bird's eye view of the tiny horseshoe-shaped cove.

The news vendor outside the underground station had one last copy of *Teen Romance*. Clutching her purchase, Lucy headed back towards the tower block. She couldn't get the magazine article out of her mind.

Amber and crimson light was streaming from the two gothic-arched stained glass windows which flanked the entrance to the tiny Roman Catholic church, which sat in the shadow of Churchill Tower. It was one of the City's few places of worship which hadn't been destroyed by the Blitz. Its studded pine doors were swung open invitingly.

Lucy entered just as the late-afternoon Mass was starting. There were only five in the congregation for the short service. She took a seat in the back row of the pews.

Prayers came with great difficulty for the troubled girl, who remained behind after the other worshippers had filed out. She sauntered into the adjoining side chapel, which seemed to double as a community hall. Remnants of an afternoon bingo session and empty tea cups were evident.

The young priest who had taken the service was folding and storing an altar cloth in a pine cupboard. Hanging beside the opened cupboard door was a faded print of a painting which Lucy recognised from her art studies in Switzerland, as the work of the

17th century Italian master Michelangelo Caravaggio. It was a bleak and brooding piece. It showed a small group of mourners, sombrely standing before an open grave in a gloomy stone crypt. They were watching two gravediggers bury a lifeless female figure. She recoiled with horror at the size of the gravediggers, one of whom had a shock of black curly hair.

'Strange composition, is it not?' The priest was now standing beside her, also gazing at the picture.

'What is its title, Father?'

'*The Burial of St Lucy*'. The girl felt herself go cold and she began to feel faint. 'The caption there at the side explains the legend'. As the priest began to read aloud, Lucy felt her body temperature falling.

"This famous altar piece depicts the martyrdom of the 4th century noblewoman Lucia of Syracuse, who swore a vow of chastity and gave away all her possessions to the poor. Her generosity so incensed the authorities that they ordered her public execution and burial. One version of the story is that she was not even dead when she was buried."

As he finished reading the caption, the priest swung the door of the vestments cupboard firmly shut. The loud click of the latch echoed around the tiny hall. Lucy suddenly recalled the imprisoning snap of the rear door of the hatchback. She moved from the priest's side and slumped down on a pew.

'Are you alright, my child?'

She hung her head in shame. 'No, Father. I feel very faint. May I rest here for a few moments?'

'But of course. Let me fetch you a glass of water.'

Lucy couldn't bring herself to look at the Caravaggio again. Its reminder of her abduction was vividly clear. The priest returned and offered the glass to the frail girl, who was quietly sobbing.

This Damascene moment seemed to lift the opaque veil which had shrouded her past life. 'You see, Father: I now know that I am

Lost Lucy!' Handing him the empty glass she walked slowly towards the church door.

The priest followed her, calling out: 'Why not stay a little longer?' But she was gone.

Lucy crossed the street and took a short cut through the Barbican's Wren Crescent, linking the symphony hall with the piazza. She knew she had to be back in the apartment before 6 and couldn't afford to risk being spotted in the reception lobby by Malcolm X, who would almost certainly report the incident to her father. 'I am NOT an orphan!' she mumbled to herself angrily.

As she skirted around the lake and headed towards the entrance to the tower's service area, she saw the red glow of a cigarette in the alcove of a fire exit beside the ramp leading to the basement. She guessed that it was Malcolm X having a crafty smoke. It meant she could risk walking through the unattended reception lobby, saving precious minutes, and take the passenger lift to the 37th floor.

Standing alone in the lobby awaiting the lift, Lucy punched a fist into the palm of her other hand. 'And I'm NOT an orphan!'

Audrey was waiting impatiently in the apartment doorway. 'Wherever have you been, child? I was starting to get worried.'

As casually as possible the girl replied: 'I met a friend from school' and strolled into the kitchen holding her new copy of *Teen Romance*.

'Well not a word of this to your dad, understand? You'll get me the sack.'

'Sorry Audrey. Mum's the word. Promise.'

As the old woman waddled towards the lift, Lucy called from the doorway: "Audrey, I don't suppose you could lend me £5 could you?"

'Of course, my lovely. Help yourself to my housekeeping cash – it's in a jar in the cutlery draw in the kitchen. Your supper's on a tray on the top. Your favourite – spaghetti rings. Just warm it in the microwave.'

As soon as she saw the lift door close, Lucy went into her bedroom and turned on her laptop computer. She figured she had about two hours to do some internet research as her father had spoken of visiting his club, which invariably meant a late return.

The official website of La Coveta Perla was disappointingly bland, filled with details of special offers, winter rates and road directions, though a high-level panoramic picture of the Aphrodite Terrace Restaurant at night gave her nasty goose pimples.

She needed confirmation that she really had been there as a child. She decided to try Google Earth and clicked on the topmost icon on her screen saver, tapping the hotel's Spanish postcode into the 'Visit' box which had appeared. The vertiginous feeling of zooming from outer space down to Europe, then Spain, then Andalusia was almost heart-stopping. It was how Alice must have felt when she fell down the rabbit hole, Lucy thought.

The satellite photographs of the Spanish resort and its little cove were pin sharp and far superior to those on the hotel's website. But Lucy wanted to get closer, focussing on the area around the Aphrodite Terrace, with its sun umbrellas erected. Beyond the statue of Aphrodite, she picked out a tall laurel hedge that led towards a long flight of steps, with the waves in the cove at the bottom twinkling invitingly. And if one final detail was needed to convince the girl that she had indeed descended those steps, there they were: great billowing swathes of purple bougainvillea.

~ ~ ~ ~ ~

At Bath Square, Chelsea, Aamir Kashani took the lift back down to the entrance hall in an irritable mood. He had decided to take a taxi to his club in Pall Mall, where he intended to order a small sandwich and a large whisky. Displaying one of the finest Anatolian pieces he had ever handled, on a tiled floor you could probably buy in any suburban bathroom centre, rankled with this traditionalist.

In his club's Library at 8.15 p.m. (and two large whiskies later), the Pakistani entrepreneur was studying the *Financial Times* when he heard the muffled ping of an incoming text message. As he moved out onto the Gallery a member who had heard the signal ostentatiously ruffled his newspaper in annoyance, remarking, in an audible stage whisper to a fellow member: 'The day the membership committee approved the application of that curry baron, certainly proved to be open season for Johnny Foreigner, didn't it?'

Seated on a leather banquette beneath a bust of Gladstone, Kashani furtively checked his mobile phone. The message read: *His Royal Highness is willing to purchase your carpet. Please advise what discount you are prepared to give. We will be paying in euros.*

He momentarily stared at the screen in disbelief, before angrily tapping in his reply: *£20,000 is the stated price. Tell His Royal Highness the currency is immaterial and that we do not give discounts. Prix fixe, as French restaurants have it.* He might have lost a sale, but his professional reputation remained unsullied.

The phone also showed a missed call. He rang it back.

'Aamir, did you call me?'

'Yes, Carla. I'm at my club. I wondered if I could call round.'

'Not tonight, sweetie. I'm all in. I've been working all day.'

'Where?'

'Lancaster House. At the big international security conference.'

'I read about it. So why were you there, darling? Have you moved into the arms trade?'

'My agency is providing ten girls as escorts for some of the overseas delegates.'

'Was Blair there?'

'*Certainmente.* Schmoozing and networking like a good 'un. Cosying up to the Azerbaijani delegation.'

The carpet dealer snorted. 'The country of choice for kleptocratic crooks and despots, according to Dame Margaret Hodge.'

'As a matter of fact, I've only just got in from the evening reception.'

'Please Carla. Just a quickie?'

'Oh, very well. But you can't stay the night, I need my beauty sleep. And by the way, Aamir, I've got some good news: I think I've sold your Sumerian vase. The one with the three grazing gazelles.'

'Really? Who to?'

'This Azerbaijani arms dealer I've been with all afternoon. He was just leaving when he spotted it in the hall. Darling, his eyes popped out on stalks! "Wherever did you find that?" he asked. "That's an incredibly rare piece."'

Kashani sat bolt upright on the bench. 'So what did you tell him?'

'I said I'd inherited it from my grandfather who was an archaeologist who'd worked in Iraq.'

'What did he say to that?'

'He asked me where my grandfather's dig had been.'

'And what did you tell him?'

I said I was only a kid at the time, but I remember receiving a postcard from Uruk.'

'Good girl! And he believed you?'

'By the look of disbelief on his face, I very much doubt it. But he knows his stuff. He's really keen to buy it. I told him I'd think it over. Usual commission?'

'Just remind me what that is, Carla? Ten per cent isn't it?'

'No it bloody-well isn't, Aamir, and you know it. It's fifteen per cent.'

He smiled. 'Silly me. Right, I'll be with you shortly and we'll decide how much he's going to pay.'

Puffing on a Havana cigar, Kashani walked from his club along Pall Mall towards Carla's apartment in St James's. He reflected how singularly ironic it was that a rare 12th century Sumerian vase, illicitly excavated by a German archaeologist, stolen from the Iraq

Museum of Antiquities and owned by a Pakistani carpet dealer, was now going to be purchased from an Italian prostitute by an Azerbaijani arms dealer who would be returning it to Asia. 'What goes around comes around,' he mused to himself.

He crossed the road in front of the old wine merchants and headed for a narrow street at the bottom of St James's. Carla's small second floor apartment (which Kashani owned) overlooked Green Park. He had always thought it had been one of his shrewdest investments, for while St John's Wood, Hampstead and even Knightsbridge were now blighted by the influx of foreign *nouveaux riche* and money launderers, St James's had remained one of the last bastions of old-fashioned affluence.

The apartment's interior was like a Parisian tart's parlour: flowery, over-decorated and smelling of Chanel No 5. But Carla's clients loved it.

As she pecked him on the cheek, Kashani's mistress growled: 'Aamir – you've been smoking cigars. I've told you how I hate having sex when you smell of tobacco. That Old Spice you wear is bad enough!'

She was clad in a very fetching Japanese kimono, which Kashani himself had bought her as a Christmas present from Liberty. He moved to unfasten its sash. 'It's only going to be a quickie, my love. You don't even need to get undressed.'

This prelude to their lovemaking was cut short by the trill of Carla's mobile phone in her bedroom. Answering the call she strolled back into the living room, gesticulating with one finger at the phone and switching it to loudspeaker mode. 'To tell you the truth, I haven't really decided on a price. Why the hurry, darling?'

A voice with a heavy accent could be heard at the other end: 'Because tomorrow I must return to Baku. If I am to buy your vase, I shall need to make a bank withdrawal in the morning.'

'As I told you, the vase has very strong sentimental attachments.' Carla looked anxiously at Kashani, who pulled a small notebook from his pocket and scribbled the figure "£60,000" in large letters across a page. 'But seeing it's you and because of the very special time we had this afternoon, I'd be prepared to take...shall we say... £60,000. GBP.'

'Halve it and I might be interested'.

'No way!'

'£45,000.'

'But the provenance – I told you it once belonged to my grandfather.'

'The provenance you speak of Miss Ponti is a *chimera*.'

Carla looked helplessly at Kashani for reassurance. He was becoming impatient. 'A *chimera*? Sorry, I don't follow.'

'If I'm about to invest so much money in a rare artefact like your vase, my dear, you would expect me to do some research, would you not?'

'So?'

'So I suggest you visit your local reference library and consult a book called *The Looting of the Iraq Museum, Baghdad*. £45,000 – and that's my final offer.'

Aamir Kashani was infuriated. Twice in less than twelve hours he had suffered the indignity of being haggled with by foreigners. He made a horizontal chopping gesture with one hand.

'Sorry, sweetie, no can do. Now it's well past my bedtime. Got to get some shut-eye. *Addio caro*.' Carla ended the call and flipped the cover down.

Picking up his gloves from the hall table, Kashani glanced at his Sumerian vase. 'I think I'll send Roland round tomorrow to collect it and take it back to Shoreditch. I wouldn't put it past that reptile to tip off the authorities before he flies out. In my experience those people don't like being thwarted. Now I must go. I told Roland to wait for me outside the side door of the Ritz. I'll be in touch.'

X

Escape Plan

'I THINK I should like to go shopping at Harrods, father', Lucy announced the following morning, as Aamir Kashani was finishing his breakfast. She had slept listlessly and wanted to put the memories created by the magazine article and the incident in the chapel as far as possible from her mind.

'I need to buy a pink clutch bag for Sandra's birthday party next Saturday.'

'Very well. I have an invitation from some city bankers to their hospitality box at the Test Match, so we can travel together. I'll get Roland to drop me off at The Oval first, then he can take you to Harrods. But we'll need to leave by 11 in case the traffic is bad.'

He handed her two £20 notes. 'Let's count this as part of your twelfth birthday present next week, shall we? If that isn't sufficient for the bag, get Roland to pay the rest and I'll settle up with him tonight.' With the three £10 notes she already had hidden in her purse (together with the £5 'loan' from Audrey) Lucy was confident she had sufficient funds for her ambitious project.

The traffic was as bad as Kashani had predicted and the final half-mile across Vauxhall Bridge was covered at a snail's pace. Crowds of pedestrians were headed towards the cricket ground. As the Lexus approached the distinctive red brick outline of the Oval's main pavilion, they saw a big trade union protest meeting was being held in front of the railings to the ground, to which giant UNITE banners had been fixed. It read: BREXIT – LET'S HAVE AN EXIT

THAT WORKS FOR WORKING PEOPLE! The union leader Len McCluskey was preparing to address the crowd.

'Let me out here, Roland, I'd rather not go anywhere near that rabble. Then take Miss Lucy to Harrods, but be sure to remain with her at all times.'

The Pakistani businessman alighted from the car, skirted around the union meeting and was soon lost in the crowd. By the time he reached his allotted hospitality box and made himself known to his hosts, the players were leaving the pitch for the lunch interval. He stepped out onto the balcony and rang Tomas Pavlovic at the warehouse.

'Have the Arabs confirmed whether they want the Oushak?'

'Not yet, Mr Kashani.. It's been very quiet this morning. Miss Remington rang from Bath Square and asked if you would ring her after 2 p.m. I've nearly finished unpacking and indexing the Stansted consignment.'

'Everything in order?'

'As far as I can see.'

'Good. Now I must go and join my hosts for lunch. I'll call you this afternoon.'

Kashani's Serb assistant put down the phone and went across to a long work bench, lit by overhead neon tubes. A white cylindrical container two metres long lay along the bench. He removed the cap from one end and slid out an Afghan rug which he carefully unrolled. Inside several layers of white kapok were six small objects, each protected by bubble wrap, labelled in black felt tip in Urdu. Without inspecting the contents, he carefully placed them on his boss's desk in the alcove. Then he started to check the carpets and rugs against the importer's manifest in order to log them onto the computer.

At the luncheon at the cricket ground, Kashani was irked to find that he was seated between Ken Livingstone, the former Mayor of

London, and Sir Nicholas Soames. The two bickered incessantly. The MP had arrived late and complained about the small size of the portions: two tiny lamb chops with redcurrant jelly and a single duchess potato, decorated with parsley. 'Did the caterers think they were feeding pygmies?' boomed the trencherman.

Play resumed promptly at 1.40 p.m. and Kashani was glad to leave his fellow guests to 'network', while he went onto the balcony to support his countrymen. At 2 p.m. precisely, he called Deirdre Remington's mobile phone.

'I'm sorry to have to tell you that the Saudis don't want to purchase your Anatolian piece after all, Mr Kashani. It seems they were offended by your inflexibility on the price.'

'And, quite frankly, I was appalled by their lack of taste, Miss Remington. Ripping up a perfectly serviceable eighty-year-old parquet floor, in my book, is sheer vandalism.'

'I hear what you say, Mr Kashani. But our Arab clients always like to drive a hard bargain. It's part of their culture.'

'Well it's no skin off my nose.' The merchant calculated that the profit he hoped to take off the Azerbaijani arms dealer - even with Carla's cut - exceeded any lost profit from the sale of the Oushak to the distasteful Arabs by a factor of more than three. Ending the call to Miss Remington courteously, he decided to enjoy the cricket for two hours, expecting his chauffeur to be parked up and waiting for him at the tea interval.

~ ~ ~ ~ ~

In Knightsbridge, Roland and Lucy eventually completed the purchase of a quilted pink clutch bag with a chrome chain shoulder strap. The chauffeur consulted his phone in case his employer had decided to leave the cricket early. Thankfully, there were no missed calls. Lucy and her minder wandered out of the store's Teen Fashion Emporium, passing a large Ladies Hair Salon.

'Roland d'you suppose I've got time to go in there and have a shampoo and cut?'

'How long would you be, Miss?' the chauffeur asked nervously.

'Well if they could fit me in straight away, no more than an hour. Shall we check?' Lucy's 'escape strategy' was being formulated minute-by-minute.

The helpful receptionist said Lucy could go in immediately and assured Roland that he could return to collect her at 2.45 p.m. The driver knew his cricket rules and regulations and reckoned that Kashani would want to be picked up from the Oval at 3.40 sharp. They should make Kennington comfortably in less than an hour. So he agreed to the arrangement and sauntered off in search of a cafeteria.

Clad in a three-quarter length white gown, Lucy was escorted down the salon to the furthest position. She easily engaged in small talk with Bianca, the pretty young assistant she had been assigned. They started with pop music and favourite singers, then moved onto the latest blockbuster movies they wanted to see. They both idolised Adele. Bianca said she was going with five other girls on a Hen Weekend to Corfu. As the girl finished combing her long auburn hair prior to washing it she asked: 'Fancy a couple of highlights?'

Lucy's reaction was cautious. 'I'm not sure. What colour?'

'What colour's the handbag you bought?'

'Pink.'

'Then how about two pinks with a crimson streak in between? It'll look really cool.' Bianca pulled her colouring trolley up to the chair and grinned into the mirror. She started rolling the foil colouring sleeves.

Lucy hesitated. 'I'm not sure if father...' but she didn't finish the sentence. She smiled to herself. What difference would it make — her father wouldn't be seeing her highlights! 'OK, but can I use the loo first?'

'Of course, hun. Through that white door at the end. You'll find the toilets on the landing opposite.'

Scooping up her shoulder bag and her new purchase, Lucy headed for the toilets. Beyond the connecting door to the salon, she was relieved to find a lift lobby, with a steel door marked STAFF & GOODS LIFT. She pressed her ear to the door to check if it was in use, but there was no sound. She decided it would be prudent to go down one floor by the stairs, in case one of the girls from the salon came looking for her.

Apart from a mountain of empty cardboard boxes, the lift lobby on the floor below was deserted. She pushed the call button to summon the goods lift. Soon she was on her way down to the store's cavernous basement service area. She yanked off her white gown and dumped it in a litter bin. There were several parked goods vehicles, with items being unloaded. She dropped back into the shadow of the lift shaft.

Sunlight was streaming down into the basement from the entrance arch at street level. But it was protected by an automatic barrier and from her knowledge of the tight security arrangements at the Barbican, Lucy felt sure that there would be a manned security cabin at the top of the ramp. Time was running out. Bianca would soon start looking for her errant client and Roland might return at any moment from his coffee break. He would be bound to alert her father immediately of her disappearance.

Alongside the lift was a pair of unpainted plywood doors marked: STAIR ACCESS TO REAR ENTRANCE HALL. She pushed one of the double doors and it swung open, revealing a concrete staircase. She quickly ascended the steps, arriving behind a pair of old-fashioned mahogany swing doors with brass handles and narrow inset windows. Through the glass she could make out the more traditional Harrods décor of a public street entrance, with shoppers coming and going. So long as she didn't encounter a commissionaire, her way out of the building should be easy. She cautiously pulled the heavy swing door back and slipped out. To her right was a short flight of steps leading down to the sun-lit pavement of a back street.

Lucy paused in her descent, as she spotted two chauffeurs standing on the corner of the side street, smoking and chatting. The one with his back to her had the same build as Roland. The man swung around to flick his cigarette end into the gutter and the girl was relieved to see that it wasn't her father's driver. At that very moment, Roland was returning to the second floor hairdressing salon to collect her.

Lucy walked to the corner of the street and waited until she spotted a vacant taxi. The driver was assisting an elderly lady from the back. He was an older man and appeared courteous and attentive. Not a bit like the shaven-headed louts with tattooed arms who pulled up in front of Churchill Tower.

'Are you free?' Lucy enquired nervously when he had finished.

'Certainly, Madam. Where would you like to go to?'

'Which railway station do I need for trains to Bristol?'

'Paddington, Madam.'

She moved to open the back door of the cab, determined to quit Knightsbridge as quickly as possible. 'Right – can we go there please?'

'Certainly Madam.' Her well-executed 'break-out' had been far easier than Lucy had expected.

As they drove northwards, Lucy tried to calculate how long she would have to get on board a Bristol-bound train before Roland raised the alarm. Probably half-an-hour at the most. The traffic was flowing freely.

After passing several terraces of well-kept Bayswater apartment blocks, the taxi drove into a long glass-roofed tunnel, where a queue of empty taxis was lined up. 'Here we are Madam. I'm afraid you've got a rather long walk to the platforms. Have you got your ticket?'

'Not yet.'

'Then follow the overhead signs saying TICKET SALES.' She paid and tipped him and thanked him for the advice. 'Visiting friends in Bristol, are you?'

'A relative actually.'

'Well have a safe journey, young lady.'

~ ~ ~ ~ ~

Roland considered saving the news of Lucy's disappearance until he had picked up Kashani at the Oval. He didn't enjoy the prospect of being roasted over his mobile phone in the lobby of Harrods, but knew that he had to face the music.

The England team was already on the field when Pakistan's Asad Shafiq and Younis Khan walked to the wicket after the lunch interval.

In the Oval hospitality box coffee was being served. Soames and Livingstone were now chatting amiably, sharing mutual reminiscences about Princess Diana. 'Such a lovely young woman. Such a great loss.' recalled the MP. 'But you know she had a bitch of a step-mother: Diana used to refer to her as "Acid Raine." He roared with laughter at his own remark. 'A social climber *sans pareil*.'

Aamir Kashani rose from the table as his mobile phone rang and stepped out onto the balcony. He checked the screen and saw that the incoming call was from his chauffeur. As he took the call, Shafiq disdainfully flicked Chris Woakes over mid-wicket for four runs. The batsmen didn't even move from their creases.

'Roland? Where are you?'

'At Harrods, Mr Kashani.'

'What the devil are you doing there? You're supposed to be parked outside the Oval!'

'There's been a slight... problem at this end, Sir.'

'Problem? What kind of problem? Did you get clamped?'

'Er no, Sir. It's just that Miss Lucy's... gone missing?'

'MISSING? How on earth could she have gone missing, man? I told you not to let her out of your sight!'

'After we'd bought the handbag, she said she wanted to have her hair done. For the party next Saturday…'

'SO?'

'So the salon booked her in and told me to come and collect her within the hour.'

'AND?'

'And when I went back to fetch her - after no more than 45 minutes, Sir - they said she'd asked to use the ladies' toilets and had never returned.'

'So what have you DONE, Roland?'

'That's why I'm ringing you, Sir. For instructions,' the driver answered plaintively.

'Go to the nearest Information Point. Ask to be directed to their Security Suite. When you get there, demand to see the person in charge. Don't be fobbed off with jobsworths or lackeys. Tell them they must immediately institute a search of the entire building, with all the security guards on the exit doors to be given her description. Have you got that?'

'I think so, Mr Kashani.'

'I'm going to put in a call to one of Harrods' directors who's a member of my club. Call me back in ten minutes with a full report. No longer, UNDERSTAND?'

'Yes, Sir.' As he closed the lid of his Nokia phone, Roland half expected to find it had melted.

The chauffeur duly rang back ten minutes later. 'They've alerted all their door security staff, but are saying they need a picture of Miss Lucy. And the manager wants you to ring him to confirm that the police can be notified'.

'Drive straight over to St Broderick's and ask the headmistress for a copy of Lucy's picture from their school records. Get her to email it to Harrods. Have you got that, Roland?'

'Yes Sir.'

'Then come and pick me up from The Oval,' he snapped.

~ ~ ~ ~ ~

At Paddington, Lucy waited patiently in the cordoned-off zig-zag ticket queue, eventually arriving at a vacant window. 'Single to Bristol, please.'

'£30. But it's better value to get a return, love,' said the cheery ticket clerk. 'Single tickets work out more expensive.'

Lucy slid three £10 notes under the window.' But you see… I'm not coming back!'

From the overhead information screens, she had ascertained the departure time of the next Bristol train and, along with a huge swathe of homeward-bound commuters, was headed for a line of intimidating automatic ticket barriers. She held back to study the routine for getting through these unfriendly-looking gates, before cautiously stepping forward to take her turn.

Everyone was rushing along the platform as if their lives depended on it. "WOULD PASSENGERS INTENDING TO TRAVEL ON THIS SERVICE PLEASE BOARD THE TRAIN AS IT IS READY TO LEAVE."

Close to where Lucy had just passed through the barrier, two armed policemen were surveying commuters coming up onto the station's concourse from the Underground. They simultaneously focussed on a young Asian backpacker. A bleep on the tablet of one of the officers alerted him to an incoming message. He took the instrument from his bullet-proof waistcoat and illuminated the screen.

MISSING CHILD ALERT. LUCY KASHANI. 12-YRS. HT:120CMS. PALE-SKINNED CAUCASIAN. BLUE EYES. AUBURN HAIR WITH SHORT PIGTAIL. WEARING BLACK PLEATED MINISKIRT, BLUE FLEECY JCKT, PINK TRAINERS. PICTURE FOLLOWS. Without taking his eyes off the youth, the officer held out the tablet for his colleague to read, murmuring 'MISPER'.

Midway along the line of carriages, Lucy spotted an elderly lady trying valiantly to manhandle a wheeled suitcase up the step into the carriage. For one dreadful moment, Lucy thought the old lady's ribbon-decked Panama hat was about the fall between the train and the platform edge.

She stopped and offered to help her and they eventually carried the case aboard like stretcher bearers. The woman slumped down into a reserved window seat. 'Come and sit next to me, why don't you, dear?' she offered. 'Haven't you got any luggage?' Lucy shook her head. She gratefully took her place beside the old woman only moments before the train pulled out of the station.

'My, my, well wasn't that a close call?' observed her companion, as the express train passed the Royal Oak marshalling yards and sped out towards the Berkshire countryside. The old lady leaned across and in a half-whisper told Lucy: 'A lot of these passengers will be getting out at the first stop, so after that I'll pop down to the buffet car to get us both a snack. Are you hungry?'

With all the excitement of her escape from Harrods, Lucy had forgotten that it was many hours since she had eaten breakfast. 'Famished!'

The old lady smiled. 'I'm Amelia Wantage, by the way. Miss Wantage. I used to be Headmistress of a girls' school in Malvern. And before I was promoted I was the music teacher.' She reached for a laminated card in a pouch fixed to the back of the seat in front of her. 'Now what do you fancy? They do some very nice hot dishes on this service. I travel to Bristol quite often. My nephew lives there. How about a grilled cheese and chutney bap, perhaps? Or a bacon roll?' She passed the card to Lucy, who eventually settled for an egg and cress sandwich and an orange smoothie.

As soon as the train had departed from Reading, Miss Wantage set off in search of the buffet car. Lucy sat very still, with her head turned towards the window. The last thing she wanted now was to be cross-examined by a ticket inspector.

The old teacher returned some ten minutes later carrying two small brown paper carriers.

'And whereabouts in London do you live, my dear?' the school teacher enquired at the end of their meal.

'In the City, in the Barbican.'

'The Barbican? I say, how very smart. I have a friend who teaches at the Guildhall School of Music. I expect you know it'.

'Yes,' replied Lucy enthusiastically, 'I've been attending their Saturday musical appreciation classes. I hope to join their Junior Music Course. Then I intend to apply for a scholarship.'

'Really? With a view to studying which instrument?'

'The cello.'

'How wonderful! Such a beautiful instrument, don't you think?'

'I do. My heroine is Jacqueline du Pré.'

Miss Wantage's eyes widened with pleasure. 'What a magical talent.'

'I've just bought a second-hand cello on the internet. It's only a German carbon cello and I'm still not very proficient yet. Are you familiar with them?'

'Yes, I am. Strange-looking things, aren't they?'

'I agree, but it has a lovely tone. Dad's promised to buy me a Strad for my 18th birthday - that's if I get into the GSM.'

'A Stradivarius? Your father must have a good job! What does he do?'

'He's an expert in oriental carpets and rugs.'

'How fascinating. Now if you will excuse me, Lucy, I shall slip down to the Ladies to powder my nose, before the train gets to Swindon.'

Though Lucy was now considerably more relaxed and thankful for the food, she was still apprehensive about the next phase of her escape mission: how to locate a Bristol care home when she hadn't even got its address.

Refreshed, Miss Wantage returned after five minutes, determined to continue their musical dialogue. 'Well, young lady, as you are no doubt something of a du Pré scholar, do you know what Jackie's favourite instrument was?'

Lucy thought for a minute. 'Well I'm pretty sure it was a Strad, because she played one on the Elgar recording. But I don't know its full title.'

'The Davidov Stradivarius. And do you know where it is now?'

'I've no idea. In a museum?'

'No. She made a provision in her Will shortly before she died to ensure that it would always be played. It is now used by the Chinese cellist Yo-Yo Ma. Did you know she studied at the GSM?'

'Yes, I did. That's why I'm determined to go there.'

'Do you live in one of those big towers?'

'Yes. Churchill Tower.' Gazing through the carriage window, Lucy enviously studied an estate of low-rise houses. 'It can be very lonely up at the top.'

'What floor are you on?'

'Thirty-seven. With very secretive neighbours. There's only three flats on each landing, you see. When Father is out all day, often the only person I see is Audrey.'

'Is Audrey your sister?'

'No, my father's housekeeper. Sometimes he doesn't get in until late and I eat my supper on a tray just watching TV.'

'Aren't there any social clubs for young people in the Barbican?'

'I'm not allowed out on my own.'

The old music teacher seemed surprised. 'Never?'

Lucy recalled her illicit excursion the previous afternoon to buy her *Teen Romance*. She shook her head. 'Not officially. I get taken to school and collected each day by our chauffeur and at weekends I only go out with my father.'

The train started to slow for the approaches to Swindon, where many passengers were preparing to get off. A tower almost as tall as Churchill Tower loomed above the station's platforms.

'Only about another quarter of an hour', the music teacher assured her companion as their train pulled into Bath Spa. 'Have you got someone to meet you at Temple Meads?'

'Err no.'

'So where are you headed to next in Bristol?'

'Somewhere called Clifton.'

'Ah yes, up by the famous suspension bridge. And are you going to visit a friend?'

'A close relative.'

The insalubrious suburbs of Bristol started to line the track as the InterCity 125 reduced its speed. The old lady looked up from her crocheting and glanced out of the window. 'I think we'll shortly be at our destination, Lucy'.

'What's the painting up the side of that building?' the girl asked as the train passed slowly by a semi-derelict office block, with a full-length graffiti work painted up its concrete façade.

'That, my dear, is a Banksy.'

'What's a "Banksy"?'

'He's Bristol's most famous artist.'

The black and red design extended the full height of the building's five storeys. It showed the silhouette of a pig-tailed girl, being carried aloft by a cluster of five red balloons, each bearing a single white letter or numeral. The coded message read: "J C 4 P M".

'He always does his paintings at night. Then disappears before anyone can catch him.' The old teacher giggled. 'Isn't it priceless?

'Back in 2009 there was a major exhibition at the city's principal art gallery, called *Banksy versus Bristol*. It featured more than 100 of his art works which had never been seen before. Do you know, over a quarter of a million people turned out to see the show? There were queues down Whiteladies Road every single day! My nephew Alex stood in the pouring rain for two hours.'

Chuckling at her Banksy reminiscence, Miss Wantage stood up to retrieve her umbrella and hat from the overhead luggage shelf and glanced out of the carriage window. 'I think we'll soon be arriving; there's the canal. I really think I should take you through the ticket barrier, my dear. Temple Meads can be an awfully intimidating place if you've never been there before. Their automatic ticket barriers are like the Hampton Court maze – nothing as orderly as those at Paddington. So when we get off the train just follow me. Then I'll show you the taxi rank. Have you got the address of the relative you're visiting?'

'Sort of.'

They alighted from the train, pulling the teacher's suitcase between them and negotiated the barriers, which were flanked by a pair of female British Transport Police Officers, wearing yellow high-visibility jackets. One was busily studying the text of a message on her mobile phone.

Then out into the afternoon sunshine which was lighting up the station forecourt. Miss Wantage vigorously waved her umbrella at a red Mini in the central parking area. 'There's Alex. Now you're sure we can't give you a lift up to Clifton?'

'That's very kind of you but I'll be fine,' Lucy replied. They shook hands and the girl nervously headed for the leading taxi on the rank.

A young Indian driver was standing beside it. The final phase of her escape plan was about to begin.

'Where to Miss?'

'Well I'm not really sure. I need to go to the district known as Clifton. But I'm afraid I haven't got the precise address of the property I'm looking for.'

'No worries,' he replied cheerily, holding the back door open for her. 'Let's get you up to Clifton.'

'May I sit in the front with you?'

'For sure. I'm Sami, by the way.'

'Pleased to meet you Sami. I'm Lucy.'

XI

Reunion

'SO WHAT EXACTLY is it that we're looking for up in Clifton?' the young Indian taxi driver asked, as he negotiated his diminutive blue Peugeot down the cobbled roadway from the railway terminus onto Temple Gate.

'A care home.'

'That's a pretty tall order.'

'Why so?'

'Because Clifton's full of care homes. There's scores of 'em. And since the area covers nearly two square miles and there's more than eighty roads, we could be driving around for the rest of the day. Haven't you got no address?'

'I'm afraid not. Though I have got a picture of the building.' Lucy pulled out her smart phone to show it to him. 'It's from a magazine article.' She enlarged the last image. The caption just said: "Residential care home in Clifton, Bristol."

He glanced across at the image. 'OK, as soon as we reach Whiteladies Road, I'll park up and take a proper look at it. You never know, I might have taken a fare there.' He turned up the volume of the car radio to catch the close of play score from the Oval.

They navigated the city centre without difficulty, then climbed the hill that led away from the City Council's crescent-shaped offices on College Green. On Whiteladies Road, Sami pulled in behind a delivery van parked in front of a Costa coffee bar. 'May I see that picture please?'

He studied it intently. 'And you say the caption said "Clifton, Bristol"?'

'Yes.'

'Not just Bristol? 'cause there's a wealth of difference.'

'No. It definitely said "Clifton, Bristol".'

'OK. But the article never gave the care home's name?'

'Nope.'

He handed the phone back to her. 'Not a lot to go on, is there? A three-storey Victorian. On a corner. There's probably dozens of buildings like that up in Clifton.'

'But not all care homes.'

'True.' He reached behind him to lift a laptop computer in its carrying case from the back seat. Setting it on his lap he folded it open. 'It's a bit of a long shot, but this could possibly make the search a little easier. Let's see what we can find on Yell.com shall we?'

A search on the internet site of the classified trade directory showed that there were fifty-four residential care homes in Clifton. 'What did I tell you?' He hurriedly scrolled down the pages, with Lucy's phone propped up at the side of the screen. 'But not all of them are showing pictures.' He finished his search and pursed his lips. 'Nope. Nothing that matches your picture.'

'Shall I pop in there and get you a coffee?' Lucy asked, gesturing to the coffee bar.

'That's very kind of you. A latte would be good. No sugars.'

'OK. I'll be right back'.

The service inside the bar was swift and the anxious girl was settled back in the front seat of the taxi within five minutes. 'Any luck?'

'Not so far. I went through the whole lot again. I've noted their postcodes and given them to Glenda.'

'Who's Glenda?'

He nodded at the dashboard. 'My bossy sat nav lady.' He sipped his coffee. 'Very unforgiving is Glenda – especially when you take the wrong exit at a roundabout. He giggled. "Turn left and left again, IMMEDIATELY!"'

Sami finished his coffee and restarted the engine. 'OK, let's get going.'

Lucy was soon to realise that the young taxi driver's observation that Clifton was full of steep-roofed three-storey Victorian villas was accurate.

She pointed at the image on her phone. 'Seems to me, Sami,' she said, after reflecting on the daunting challenge, 'that the fact that it's obviously set on a corner – in other words, the junction of two roads – could be the key. So if you follow Glenda's instructions and the property turns out to be in the middle of a row of houses, then we just drive by and ignore it.'

'Smart thinking young lady.' The driver accelerated past another non-starter. It was beginning to get dark and a light drizzle was falling.

'How many more?' Lucy asked plaintively.

'Eight.' The supreme confidence she had had back on the Temple Meads taxi rank was beginning to slowly trickle away.

Sami steered the taxi along a broad tree-lined avenue and slowed their speed as they approached a minor T-junction. But he pulled in and parked well before they had reached the intersection.

'What's up?'

He nodded up ahead at a gaunt-looking Victorian mansion set on the corner. Rain glistened on the steep slopes of its slate roof and lights were already on in several of the upstairs rooms. He switched off the engine and turned to Lucy, smiling. 'I think we might have found it.'

Lucy froze. She didn't need to glance down onto her lap. Even at twenty-five metres, every detail coincided: the pitch of the roof, the low garden wall, even the gate posts with their pyramid stone cappings.

'Stay here, Sami. I want to go and double-check.'

She slipped out and slowly crossed the wet road. The path from the entrance gate to the front door was laid in the same black-and-white checkerboard pattern as the picture had shown. And, yes, the front door even had two rectangular glass panels.

But nowhere was there a sign to indicate that this was a residential care home. Her heart sank. It looked like a rather large private house. Perhaps her earlier foreboding that the home had closed since the *Semi-Quaver* article was published was correct.

Suddenly she spotted the back of a large timber sign in the garden, set at forty-five degrees and facing the traffic junction. She cautiously walked round to read its front. "PARAGON CARE Private Residential Care Home" it announced. Looming above the pavement opposite was the distinctive dappled trunk of a large plane tree.

She returned excitedly to give Sami the news, clicking again to the image on her phone and seeing - for the first time - that the picture showed a tall tree in the background.

Her young Indian driver was thrilled by her news and even tried to reduce the huge fare which was now showing on the taxi's meter. She tipped him generously with the last of her funds.

'Why don't I just wait until you're sure this is the right place?'

But Lucy was having none of it. Her supreme confidence that she was near her journey's end had returned. Sami waved to her from his opened window as he sped down the road back to Temple Meads Station.

She crossed the road and walked confidently up the front path. She rang the door bell. Eventually it was opened by a stout middle-aged nurse, who looked quizzically at the youngster. 'Can I help you?'

'I should like to visit Mrs Doreen Wilmot, please.'

'You'd better step inside.'

The brightly-lit hall smelt strongly of disinfectant. To the immediate right, an opened door revealed a communal lounge, in which a number of elderly people, all seated in armchairs, were sitting watching a quiz programme on TV. Beside the staircase was an opened panelled door marked MATRON.

'You say you've called to visit Mrs Wilmot?'

'That's right.'

'And what is your relationship to her?'

'I'm a relative. A close relative.'

'I have to be extremely careful in the case of this patient, Miss…?'

'Jones.'

'…Miss Jones. Because the lady in question does not receive visitors. She is extremely frail. It's doctor's orders, you see.'

'Then may I see the doctor?'

'Dr Barlow is not here. He's a senior consultant at the Royal Bristol Infirmary in the city. He only comes up here twice a week – as our consultant physician - to carry out his routine visits.'

Lucy was becoming frustrated by this obstructive woman. After her escape from Harrods, the train journey and the two-hour search in Sami's taxi, she was in no mood to be thwarted at the eleventh hour. 'So when's he next due to come here?'

'Next Tuesday.' The answer was given with the sort of finality that indicated that the interview was about to be ended.

But Lucy was far from done. 'Would you be so kind as to contact Dr Barlow by telephone?'

The Matron gave a gimlet-like glare at this impertinent girl and was about to deliver a crushing riposte when Lucy added: 'As you said yourself a moment ago, Matron, he is this care home's consultant physician. I should have thought that the well-being of one of its patients was of paramount importance. And certainly shouldn't be delayed for four days.'

The woman pursed her lips. Was there any other delaying tactic she could use to get rid of this tiresome girl? 'Actually, we will shortly be serving the patients' evening meal in the lounge. This is all most inconvenient. Can't it wait until next week?'

Lucy remained calm and courteous – though inwardly she was fuming. 'I have travelled down from London specifically to see my... to see Mrs Wilmot. I would really appreciate it if you would call Dr Barlow. I will sit here in the hall and read a magazine until he gets here from the hospital.' So saying, she picked up a dog-eared copy of *Home and Beauty* and moved to sit on a bench by the front door. Lucy decided that the 'finality' ploy could be used by both sides.

With an audible sniff the Matron said: 'Very well', turned on her heel and walked into her office, closing its door.

~ ~ ~ ~ ~

It was nearly 9 o'clock in the evening when Lucy looked up to see the headlights of a car through the glass panels of the front door. She heard a door slam shut and then footfalls up the tiled path, followed by a ring on the door bell.

The Matron appeared from the lounge to admit Dr Barlow. He was a tall distinguished West Indian man in his mid-sixties, with a balding head. He nodded politely at Lucy but didn't offer any greeting. The Matron hustled him into her office, closing the door. A full twenty minutes elapsed before the Matron reappeared.

'Miss Jones? Would you come this way? Dr Barlow would like to have a chat with you.' Lucy was ushered into the office and was relieved to note that the overbearing woman left the two of them alone. She took a seat beside the desk. Barlow studied an opened file on the desk in front of him for several minutes, before closing it. He clasped his hands together and smiled at Lucy.

'Matron says that you are a close relative of Mrs Wilmot.'

'That is correct, doctor.'

'And that you have travelled down from London especially to see the patient.'

'Yes.'

'When was the last time you saw Mrs Wilmot?'

Lucy paused for a long time. She lowered her head and closed her eyes. She saw Diane and Geoff Evans and Anna, seated together at a dinner table. Spanish music was playing. Her mother was leading her by the hand towards an apartment building.

'When I was six.'

Dr Barlow re-opened the file and turned back its sheets to the opening page, which appeared to be a photocopy of a news item from a tabloid newspaper. He smiled at what he read, closed the file and looked up at the girl seated across the desk from him. 'What an interesting answer you just gave.'

'Because?'

'Because you could have said: "Not for more than six years". Or even "not since 2009". Instead, Lucy, you told me (confirming a strange premonition I had when I was coming up from the city) your age when you and your mother were separated.'

Lowering her head, Lucy began sobbing quietly. The doctor moved around the desk to comfort her and they remained silently together for several minutes.

Dr Barlow broke the silence. 'We must proceed with the utmost caution, Lucy, as I'm sure you realise. Your mother is extremely frail, having suffered a nervous breakdown some months ago. But she is still relatively young and being reunited with you could prove to be a Heaven-sent boost for her recuperation. So let us go up to the top floor together, shall we? Leave me to prepare her for your appearance. Then when I judge the moment right, I'll come to the door and usher you in to leave you alone together'.

Lucy stood on the silent landing outside the closed door of her mother's room for what seemed like an eternity. Finally, the door was opened by the kindly doctor, who nodded for her to enter. He remained in the doorway and called out: 'You have a visitor, Doreen', before slipping quietly from the room.

She saw a frail and stooped woman in a trim white nightdress seated in a wing armchair at the window, with a crocheted rug laid across her legs. Though she was half-turned away from the doorway, the neckline of her gown revealed a green jade necklace. She turned her head unsteadily in the direction of the visitor.

Lucy approached with great trepidation and stood before her. She leaned forward and took the two bony hands in hers. 'I am Lucy. Don't worry Mother I will never leave you again.'

Epilogue

LATE ON SATURDAY afternoon, Tomas Pavlovic was logging the latest Pakistan consignment onto the computer.

The familiar chimes of the BBC's main evening bulletin caught his attention and he moved across to the TV set above Kashani's desk. He sat in the boss's high-backed leather chair as a sombre-faced Fiona Bruce appeared on the screen.

'Good evening. With less than one hundred days to the US Presidential election, things are hotting up in the race for the White House, with Hillary Clinton and Donald Trump virtually neck-and-neck.' The newsreader glanced down at a slip of paper she was holding, as a 'Breaking News' ticker-tape caption simultaneously clicked across the bottom of the screen.

'In a moment we will have an election update from our North America Editor Jon Sopel. But first: there have been dramatic developments this afternoon in the case of the missing girl Lucy Wilmot, at the centre of one of the most high-profile international police searches in recent years.' A back-projected aerial image of the Barbican towers appeared behind the newsreader. 'We are going straight over to the City of London, where a statement is due to be made outside Wood Street Police Station.'

The picture on the screen showed a short flight of stone steps bathed in bright artificial light. A tall uniformed police officer, flanked by helmeted constables, stood holding a sheaf of papers. Above its gold-edged peak, the cap of the City of London Police Commissioner had a distinctive red and white checkerboard band. Three large black microphones were being held close to his chest by figures out of frame. One of them was marked Telesinco5 – the

Spanish TV channel. Adjusting his glasses, the City's most senior policeman began reading from the papers he was holding.

'Following information received last night from a care home in Bristol, officers from the City of London police raided an apartment in the Barbican at 6 a.m. this morning. They arrested a Mr Aamir Kashani, described as a dealer in oriental carpets, who was later charged here at Wood Street police station with the unlawful abduction and imprisonment of Miss Lucy Wilmot, the six-year-old English girl who disappeared in 2009 while on holiday with her parents in Spain. Mr Kashani remains in custody and will appear at Bow Street Magistrates Court on Monday morning.' Looking tired, but wearing a quiet smile of satisfaction, DI Tanner could be seen standing behind the Commissioner.

The Barbican image faded as Fiona Bruce glanced down at a note on her desk. 'The BBC understands that other charges, including the illegal importation of antiquities, may follow within the next twenty-four hours. Now over to Jon Sopel in Washington.'

Barely minutes after the bulletin had ended, a convoy of police cars and vans pulled up in front of the Shoreditch premises of Kashani Carpets.

Hearing the buzz of the street intercom, Tomas pressed the TV remote control's mute button and crossed the warehouse floor. He lifted the intercom's handset to hear: 'City of London Police. Open up: we have a warrant to search these premises.'

~ ~ ~ ~ ~

In Durham, in a small bed-sit overlooking the Wear Gorge, Andy Wilmot had witnessed the historic broadcast. As his TV picture switched to a Washington rooftop, he cut the sound to take an incoming call. Though still numbed by the news, he had a shrewd idea who was calling. It was an exultant Deborah Tanner.

'Andy? SUCCESS!'

'I've just been watching you stood next to that police chief. It was just....just BRILLIANT!'

'I can't tell you what that meant to me this afternoon. Standing there in the glare of all those arc lights beside the Commissioner.'

'I was really proud of you, Debs. Truly.'

After a long pause: 'That's really sweet of you.' Andy sensed that she was filling up. 'But it was all down to your Lucy's amazing resourcefulness. And the fact that you never EVER gave up believing. Didn't I say all along you'd be reunited?'

'You did! And you were right. So when am I going to get to see her?'

'You're going to have to be extremely patient, I'm afraid. It may be a several days before you two can meet up. She's staying with her mother at the care home in Bristol. Dr Barlow – he's the one who first raised the alarm – has arranged for Lucy to have an adjoining room. I dare say there'll be witness statements to be taken. My chief has put in a request for me to go down to take them as SIO. Bristol Social Services are on the case because of Lucy's age. I've asked them to contact you today. It'll probably be a Louise Parsons. She'll be able to tell you how Doreen is bearing up. I bet it'll do wonders for her.'

'So tell me, did you go on the Barbican raid this morning?'

'I'm afraid not. By rights the SIO normally serves the warrant, but I was driving to London from Bedfordshire. They got me out of bed at four in the morning to give me the news! Dave and Wendy are with me, by the way. Some of the team went in armed, so it wasn't really "girls' work."

'I gather our friend Black Jacket threw a full-on strop. Shouted about racially-motivated abuse of his human rights. And that scumbag has the nerve to talk about human rights! Two of our guys had to restrain him from going out onto the balcony. And as the apartment is on the 37th floor, I don't suppose he was planning to water the plants.' She giggled at the remark. 'There's lots more to come out, believe me.'

A male voice in the background could be heard calling: 'Oi! Aren't you coming Debs?'

After her initial mood of tearful elation, Deborah Tanner was now recharged. 'Andy, I'd better go. The Superintendent is taking us all to the local boozer to celebrate. And as SIO I have to get the first round in.' She called back to the male voice who had summoned her: 'I'll catch up with you, Dennis!

'Listen Andy – now that this is all out in the open, you're going to be the centre of attention; you and your daughter. I'm pretty confident that between them Bristol Social Services and the local force will shield Lucy from unwanted Press intrusion. In fact I wouldn't mind betting that Avon and Somerset has already issued formal Press guidelines. There's no way that Bristol hacks will ever get inside the Paragon Care Home in Clifton. But you're pretty vulnerable up there, you know.'

'Am I?'

'You'd better believe it, honey. The Stan Murds and Terry Danters of this world will soon smoke you out. I wouldn't mind betting there's a Tyne & Wear stringer sniffing around Durham already – probably tipped off by The Wally. Maybe I should come up. After all, as SIO I have a duty to give you a full report. I tell you, Andy: what your Lucy pulled off last Friday would do credit to Harry Houdini.' Andy rather liked the thought of his daughter as an escapologist. 'I've got a fair bit of Time Off In Lieu due to me. What say I come up to Durham next weekend? Keep you company and fend off all the Press?'

'Sounds like a plan.'

'Call me in the morning. Not too early though, as I'll probably have a hangover!'

~ ~ ~ ~ ~

Andy had a restless night. He got up at 6 a.m. and made himself a strong mug of tea. His iPhone showed seven missed calls and fifteen text messages. He scrolled down the list and opened the one from Geoff Evans.

> *Epic news! We're so thrilled for you, mate. We had to have Anna sleep with us last night as she was as high as a kite! All she keeps saying is 'Awesome!' Di desperately wants me to drive us all down to Bristol, so text me soonest when you think we could go. G. PS: Next time you're speaking to Lucy just say: 'Jack Sparrow sends his love.'*

~ ~ ~ ~ ~

Andy left it until shortly before 10 a.m. before he rang Deborah. 'So how did it go - your All Coppers knees-up?'

'It was great. What I remember of it. Dennis let me spend the night on his sofa. The City Commissioner was terrific. Stayed until the bitter end. That bloke's got hollow legs. And the stuff he came out with, Andy the tabs are going to have a field day!'

'Such as what?'

'The raid on the Shoreditch warehouse turned up a veritable can of worms, so I'm told. There will probably be a Press announcement mid-morning to catch the one o'clock news bulletins. But Dennis reckons it's matey's mistress who's going to get the most lurid headlines when she appears in court. Seems she was an inveterate bookkeeper.'

'Sorry, Debs, I'm not with you.'

'Black Jacket's mistress - Carla the Harlot. She was on the game. Kashani's going to be done for living off immoral earnings, though it's a lesser charge than the abduction one. Miss Ponti kept a little ledger of all her clients. It's in the safe at Wood Street at the moment, but the Commissioner gave us some edited highlights last night in the boozer.'

'Care to share?'

'I'm afraid it will have to wait until I come up to Durham at the weekend. "Walls have ears" nudge nudge. Suffice to say it's a veritable Debretts of Shagging: MPs, Peers of the realm, city bankers, oligarchs. Even a leading churchman.'

'How fascinating!'

'Did you sleep all right last night?'

'Not really. I stayed up to watch the late news, just in case there were any further updates, but all the channels were just re-broadcasting the City of London Police Commissioner's statement. I so want to see an up-to-date image of my daughter, Debs. Do you realise it's six years since I last saw Lucy?'

'Try to be patient for a little longer, Andy. Tell me - have you heard from Louise Parsons yet?'

'Yes. She called yesterday evening, just after I spoke to you. She said Lucy's settling in well, given all the dramas she's been through. But she wants me to hold off going down to Bristol until next week. She said Doreen's a changed woman since Lucy arrived. And Doreen's brother has come up trumps as well.'

'In what way?'

'He and his wife live in a huge house up in Clifton, which has an unused basement. He's offered to convert it into a flat for Doreen to share with Lucy. He even thinks he can pull some strings to get Lucy a place at Colston Girls' School.'

'How do you feel about that?'

'About Lucy and Doreen living together in Bristol?'

Andy Wilmot reflected for a moment. 'Yes, I think it could work. According to Miss Parsons, Dr Barlow believes Lucy's arrival could do wonders for Doreen's health.' He paused, before adding with a sigh: 'But it does rather leave me out on a limb up here on my own.'

'I could always apply for a transfer to Durham Constabulary.'

- E N D -

Nick Jones

… has spent his life connected with buildings. Initially working as a surveying assistant on a major tunnelling project under the City of London, he moved into architectural journalism, working for a publishing group which was part of Express Newspapers. He first edited specialist supplements for the weekly newspaper Building Design then later became Editor of the conservation monthly Building Refurbishment. He has contributed to many other architectural publications. His debut novel 'King's Cross' was published in August 2015. His second novel 'The Shropshire Stalker' came out in 2016. For his fourth novel, Nick has chosen the topical subject of people trafficking. It is due to be published in 2020 The writer now lives in Herefordshire.